Praise for *Ray in Reverse*

"Wallace's great gift as a writer lies in his ability to create a comic surface that somehow succeeds in exposing the essential sadness of life. *Ray in Reverse* is an emotionally persuasive novel . . . with an abundance of charm."
— *Richmond Times-Dispatch*

"Wallace follows his inventive debut novel, *Big Fish,* with another ingenious tragicomedy . . . a funny, poignant narrative that moves with the clarity of a fable and the complexity of modern psychology. . . . Wallace's stylistic tour de force, bolstered by the richness of his family portraits, humor, and appreciation of ordinary people, proves him an author of extraordinary originality, craftsmanship, and charm." — *Publishers Weekly* (starred review)

"A deft and economical writer with a fine ear for dialogue, Wallace has produced a finely wrought novel . . . building in power as this life unfurls from front to back."
— *Kirkus Reviews* (starred review)

"A delightful, small package of exquisite writing . . . Ray is real, and his life makes oddly compelling reading— especially in reverse."
— *Booklist* (starred review)

Ray in Reverse

PENGUIN BOOKS

RAY IN REVERSE

Daniel Wallace is also the author of *Big Fish*. He has published stories in numerous magazines, including *Story, Glimmer Train, Prairie Schooner, Shenandoah,* and others. Raised in Birmingham, Alabama, Wallace now lives in Chapel Hill, North Carolina, where he works as an illustrator.

Ray in Reverse

~~~ by ~~~

DANIEL WALLACE

PENGUIN BOOKS

PENGUIN BOOKS
Published by the Penguin Group
Penguin Putnam Inc., 375 Hudson Street,
New York, New York 10014, U.S.A.
Penguin Books Ltd, 80 Strand, London WC2R 0RL, England
Penguin Books Australia Ltd, Ringwood, Victoria, Australia
Penguin Books Canada Ltd, 10 Alcorn Avenue,
Toronto, Ontario, Canada M4V 3B2
Penguin Books (N.Z.) Ltd, 182–190 Wairau Road,
Auckland 10, New Zealand

Penguin Books Ltd, Registered Offices:
Harmondsworth, Middlesex, England

First published in the United States of America by Algonquin
Books of Chapel Hill, a division of Workman Publishing, 2000
Published in Penguin Books 2001

1   3   5   7   9   10   8   6   4   2

Grateful acknowledgment is made to the following magazines,
where portions of this book first appeared: *Glimmer Train,
The Quarterly, The Yale Review, Shenandoah, TriQuarterly,
Carolina Quarterly, The Boston Globe Magazine,* and *Story.*

THE LIBRARY OF CONGRESS HAS CATALOGED
THE HARDCOVER EDITION AS FOLLOWS:
Wallace, Daniel, 1959–
Ray in reverse/by Daniel Wallace.
p.   cm.
ISBN 1-56512-260-7 (hc.)
ISBN 0 14 20.0009 4 (pbk.)
1. Aging—Fiction.   2. Men—Fiction.   I. Title.
PS3573 A4256348 R39 2000
813'.54—dc21   99–088844

Printed in the United States of America
Set in Times Ten

To Joe Regal and Kathy Pories

Contents

RAY IN HEAVEN   1

SPRING 1999, HIS LAST DAYS   13

FALL 1994, THE ART OF LOVE   28

FALL 1993, AFTER SHE LEFT HIM   35

FALL 1993, HIS CALLUSES   42

SUMMER 1992, THE HOUSE HE BUILT   44

FALL 1982, RAY IN ABSENTIA   59

WINTER 1981, WHAT HE SAW   70

SPRING 1979, WORK-IN-PROGRESS   82

FALL 1976, THE MAIN THING   104

WINTER 1972, COLD FEET   136

SPRING 1969, THE DOG HE RAN OVER   148

SUMMER 1962, HIS UNCLE'S EX-WIFE   168

FALL 1961, INHERITANCE   186

SUMMER 1960, A GOOD DEED   201

RAY IN HEAVEN   221

I'd like to thank everybody at Algonquin Books and Russell and Volkening for making this book possible. I'd like to thank Abby, Lillian, and Henry—my family— for everything else.

Ray in Heaven

Ray, like the rest of us here, is dead. He sits in a folding metal chair toward the back of the group, right on the fringe, as though he is unsure of himself, of where he belongs. That's fine, he's new here, and there's always a transition from one world to the next. He doesn't know how lucky he is though! First of all, he's in Heaven, which clearly makes him at least a little special. Second, he's in Last Words. In Heaven these days Last Words is more popular than ever, so securing a place here in our group has become quite difficult. There's the waiting list, which is longer than most, and then of course the words themselves have to be of a certain caliber (there's a screening committee). Still, sometimes strings are pulled, and I wonder if this is what happened with Ray. Certainly that's why Stella Kauffman is here, this slight, pale woman with an eager, ingratiating smile, who joins us today for the first time: it was her ancestor Betty Karnovski who started the group an age or two ago, so we had to take her in.

When it's time to begin, Stella raises her hand and Betty—no surprise to me—picks her to start us off.

"I'm from New York City," Stella says, an admission that generates a little tremor through the group: New York City is so poorly represented in Heaven that some of us had forgotten it exists. Stella shifts, uncomfortable in the metal chairs provided for our group, and she squints a bit—the overhead fluorescent lights always seem too bright in the beginning—and then she clears her throat and begins.

"Okay. My last words. 'I wonder if I left the oven on.'"

She utters them to us with an operatic undertone in her voice, as though she were God. Then she settles back, satisfied apparently.

A few of us nod, but none of us dare look Stella's way: we're embarrassed for her. Her last words are dreadful. She's only been here a day, of course, and this is her first session. Still . . . they're awful. She might have waited to hear the others, might have waited to hear what proper last words sound like before she made the mistake of uttering her own. They just weren't put well, and they don't really mean anything either, and that's unfortunate. Because meaning is important in Heaven. Consider your subjects: Life. Death. An overview of the former would be nice; a

2

subtle observation of the latter, even better. Especially for somebody like Stella Kauffman—a woman from such a colorful place. Her showing is less than we would have expected. Betty is especially disappointed.

Which is not to say she had no reason to utter them, of course. Stella makes this clear to us immediately. On the night of her death she was alone, and it was a heart attack that killed her, one so sudden that it gave her very little time to recap her life experience. In fact, her last words were spoken that afternoon, three hours before she died, when she left her apartment to go for a short walk. Half a block away she remembered the oven, in which she had been baking some wonderfully delicious artery-hardening cookies, and wondered out loud whether or not she had turned it off.

"So, I said, 'I wonder if I left the oven on.' But it turned out I didn't," she says. "I mean, I did. I mean . . . the oven was off when I got home."

Everyone in the group nods, smiles, but still, we are far from impressed. Stella Kauffman must have led a very bland life indeed.

"They were my last words," she says, a note of defiance in her voice. "I like them well enough."

"As you should, Stella," Betty says. "As you should."

"Obviously they're not the best. Had I the chance to say them all over again, of course, I would do much bet . . ." she says, trailing off, realizing, as we all do rather quickly here, that this topic—the Ifs Ands and Buts of life—is one rarely explored in Heaven; and Stella, wisely, does not pursue it.

Instead, to leave us with something a bit more memorable, she describes for us what it feels like to have a heart attack.

She says, "It is like being on an elevator and having it stop between floors."

Very good indeed, Stella! I think, and warm a bit toward her: that is exactly what it was like. For me, I mean. The sudden jolt. The stopping. The darkness.

"And that's the way it still feels," she says, a bit harshly.

Well. I have a feeling Stella has some unresolved issues about dying she may need to work on, and if so, she's in the wrong place. There are other groups for that sort of thing.

I REMEMBER MY FIRST days in Last Words, as I anticipated sharing with the group. That was an age ago now, maybe more, and I was nervous. But then, everything about Heaven made me nervous at first. But my words: I knew they were good (they get better each time I tell them) but how they would stack up against the others here I just wasn't sure.

There were a number of poets in the group at that time, and I figured theirs would be among the best. But poets have not cornered the market on fine last words, not by a long shot. Generally speaking, it is their next-to-last words that are the good ones. In fact, their next-to-last words are very good indeed. They're self-conscious, I think, and ambitious; even as they die they want to turn a good phrase. Some of the poets here will admit to a little deathbed revision.

One poet, a man who goes by the initials S. J., says he was so busy mentally refining the iambic farewell he had devised that he "did not sense Death's coming" and asked his friend to make him a grilled cheese sandwich. Those were his last words. "A grilled cheese sandwich, Freddy, please."

And Freddy complied, but S. J. never got a chance to eat it: he died before the butter melted.

And now more than anything, he says, a grilled cheese sandwich is what he'd like, what he'd really like, what he can almost taste, he says, what he can't stop thinking about. He's in Unfulfilled Desires now, I think. He's working it out.

AFTER STELLA KAUFFMAN'S POOR showing Ray raises his hand.

"Ray," Betty says. "You have some last words you'd like to share with us?"

He says he does. But he prefaces his remarks by telling us that he bled to death, slowly, on a roadside near Dallas.

Ray is a tall, broad-shouldered man with a nervous energy that puts us all on edge. He's always drumming his fingers against the side of the chair, and getting up, moving around, as though he can't get comfortable. But he doesn't look like the kind of man who would bleed to death on a Texas roadside. He has a somewhat more homogenized, suburban presence, and the gaunt and darkened look of a man who does not like himself all that much. Bitter for some reason, and sad. He makes a pretty big deal about this bleeding, the last episode in his life, going on and on, but no one is really interested. No one is interested in how he died. Whether it was a gun shot or if he fell off a horse or if it was suicide, we don't really care. All I want to know is, What did you say? As you were leaking away, Ray, there by the side of the road, what were they? What were your last words?

"My brother was there," he says, milking his time for all its worth, "kneeling beside me."

An audience! Good. And a family member. Some of the best last words are often spoken in the presence of a family member. Ray was lucky; some of us died in front of total strangers, too embarrassed to say anything at all.

"We were waiting for help," he says, "but both of us knew I wasn't going to make it. I knew it, anyway. Tom kept saying, 'You're going to be okay, big brother. You're going to be just fine.' He kept talking like this, but I believe he knew it, too."

"The last words, Ray?" Betty says abruptly. She looks at her wrist where a watch used to be: force of habit.

"What? Oh, right," he says. "My last words. Well, I looked up at Tom, my baby brother, who was holding my

6

head in his hands, and I told him, 'Be sure to take care of Jenny for me.' Jenny is my wife—my widow now. 'And tell her I love her.' Loved. I said 'loved.' Yeah. Like I was dead already. Then I said, 'Besides our mother, Tom—my Jenny is the greatest, most wonderful woman I ever—"

"Ray?" Betty interrupts him.

"What?"

"Is this true? Is what you're telling us true?"

"What do you mean, true?" he says. "Of course it's true."

"Ray."

Ray shifts in his chair, wipes his nose with a monogrammed handkerchief, blinks his eyes.

"Okay," he says. "Okay. I guess I'm making it up, most of it. You know. So what?"

"That's fine, Ray. Fine. I think we understand. But would you tell us what you said? Honestly now, Ray—the truth. What was it you said to your baby brother?"

Ray squirms a little.

"I don't have a baby brother," he says. "A sister, Eloise, but no brother."

"I see," Betty says. "So you were bleeding—"

"Cancer," Ray says. Clearly, this is difficult for him, returning to his last moments alive. His eyes gaze downward, through the floor, as though he can see where he came from, that blue-green marble spinning through space. But he can't. All he can see is the floor. "I was dying of cancer." And here he displays his fingers in a way that suggests the holding of a cigarette. "My wife was there. Jenny. Her name really was Jenny. Is. My son was there, too. James. Anyway, I could tell—you know. Sometimes I guess you just know. So before I died I wanted to tell her what was in my heart, and I said 'I wish.' That was it. I said, 'I wish,' and then I died."

"Thank you, Ray," Betty says, clearing her throat, clearly relieved Ray's done with, and turning away from him to look for the next volunteer.

"Happy now?" Ray says, though his turn is clearly over. Betty looks back at him, irritated, but this doesn't stop Ray. "Those are them, the very last ones. I said it, and suddenly—I was a goner. And personally I don't think they were all that damn bad."

"No one said they were, Ray."

"Yeah," he says. "But you can tell. You can tell when everyone thinks you don't measure up, that their last words are better than yours. Why don't we talk about last thoughts for a change? Because my last thoughts were special."

"What did you wish for, Ray?" Stella asks, interrupting. Everybody looks at her as though she's insane. She tries to smile. "I mean, I'd be interested."

Betty shakes her head. Explaining, augmenting, appending: it's just not done here. But if Ray is willing, it doesn't appear that anyone is prepared to stop him. We watch him, seething in his anger, and then a shadow seems to pass over him—the look of a man revisiting his life. But then he snaps back and glares at us.

"You know what I wished?" he says. "You know what I wished? Hell, I'm not even going to tell you. You don't deserve to know."

Ray stares at Betty for a long time, and then around at our circle. We all look back at her sympathetically: he's got some issues. In life, he was probably a salesman. He was a moderately successful salesman with a family who never understood him or his reason for being. You can almost see him nursing his anger as though it were a little life itself. As though it's all he has.

"I am so happy to be in Heaven," he says. He laughs, shakes his head, and then he spits on the ground before us. "There. Yes. That's how happy I am to be in Heaven. I've got my hair back," he says, smiling bitterly, and touching it, his head, softly once, with his fingers. "That's nice. But so far that's about the only thing. My hair."

None of us has ever seen such behavior before; Betty is too stunned to speak. But Stella Kauffman, who has been here the shortest time of anybody, merely laughs.

Ray gets up and walks over to Mr. Joyce, who has been here a good part of forever.

"Tell us your last words, Mr. Joyce," Ray says to him. "I bet they were something."

Mr. Joyce is flustered; he adjusts his spectacles, then takes them off and begins to rub them with his tie. He turns to Betty Karnovski for help, but Betty is looking down. She hates this sort of conflict.

9

Mr. Joyce smiles his age-old smile.

"Why, everyone here has heard my last words, Ray."

"Then what's the problem?"

"I like to prepare," he says.

"How about just telling us the truth," Ray says.

Mr. Joyce turns red suddenly and begins to shake like the sky does when it rains.

"I have always told the truth about my last words!" he insists. "How dare you! Why would I . . ."

But then, he calms down: Stella Kauffman, we note, has laid her hand on his knee.

"Well," he says, "my last words were as follows: 'Another pillow, please, and some blankets.'"

Ah, yes. The last words of Mr. Joyce. These rank with some of the best last words in Heaven, believe it or not. There are a couple of reasons this is so. One, they smack of metaphor (which Mr. Joyce excels in). The fact is, Mr. Joyce was cold (someone had left the window open) and he needed blankets to make him warm, but the words seem to hint at something more than this, don't they? Two—and this is crucial—is the way it affected those listening bedside.

"Tears!" he has said time and again. "My God, there was a river of tears after I said that, and then when I gasped for air, and my eyes fluttered, I tell you, it brought the house down."

"Really?" Ray says—and now we all wait for what we've witnessed a thousand times before. "Come on, Mr.

Joyce," he says, "you're no different than me. That's not what you really said, is it?"

"Of course it is!"

Ray laughs and moves closer to Mr. Joyce. He's right in his face.

"I'm not convinced," Ray says, nearly whispering. "Try again."

"Fine!" Mr. Joyce says, looking away to somebody for help, but none is forthcoming. "Fine then. My actual last words were, 'For once in your life, do something right!' These to my only son. I can't even remember why I said them now, I . . . I died soon thereafter. But I cursed him with my last breath, and for that I know his life was never the same again."

Mr. Joyce begins to cry.

Ray turns on Dave McAllister, a former salesman.

"Dave," he says. "Dave. I'm sure your last words were exceptionally winning."

"I suppose so," Dave says, grinning, blushing a little. "Maybe not exactly exceptional . . ."

"Share, please," Ray says.

"Sure," Dave says. "No problem. 'And one more thing, sweetheart.' Right?" And he looks around at the rest of us for approval. These have been a longtime favorite here; I like them. They seem to typify the dying experience extremely well. "One more thing"—and the rest is . . . silence.

"But," Ray says.

"But what?"

"But, actually."

"Actually," Dave says, trying to smile. "Actually, you're right. They were slightly different. What I really said was, 'Get the hell out of my room,' or something to that effect— to my wife, I think it was. But that, you know—I didn't know I was going to die then, Ray. If I'd known . . ."

Ray shakes his head and laughs. He is disgusted with all of us. He stares at each of us, one at a time, but not one of us can look back at him. We know who we are and what it was we said.

Then he turns to me.

"And you," he says. "You."

"Me?"

"Yes. Would you like to share your oh so wonderful last words with us?"

"Well, of course, Ray," I say, shifting in my seat a bit. But Ray does not scare me. After all, what could he possibly do to me that has not already been done? "Of course, of course. My last words. I would be glad to—"

"Oh just forget it," he says, waving a dismissive hand my way. "Who needs this crap? I don't know what the big deal is anyway. Last words . . . you can have 'em! There're lots of better groups than this one. Lots!" he says and, turning, walks away from us and disappears.

SPRING 1999

His Last Days

The birds were making their nests out of Ray's hair that spring. Jenny and Ray had been saving his hair in a plastic bag for just that purpose, and it was working better than they could have imagined. Jenny had read about doing this in one of her backyard bird-watching books. She took the plastic netting the onions came in and filled it with Ray's hair and then hung the bag on the old oak tree. After only a couple of days most of it was gone. Wrens, finches, cardinals: they were all going to raise their young in his hair.

Jenny's hair was long and turning gray. Ray remembered when it had been dark brown. When her hair was down she moved it away from her face or from one shoulder to the other almost haughtily, as though her hair were a cape, or some royal designation. Her eyebrows were full and ran from one side of her face to the other, nearly meeting above her nose. In the right slant of light Ray could see an almost invisible fuzz illuminated across her cheek and on her chin line, like a tiny field of translucent wheat. Ray remembered the hair around her vagina was as soft and dense as the inside of a pillow.

It seemed that as soon as they started noticing birds is when the birds came, though they must have been here before. This was the same time last year when his hair started coming out in bunches. He quit smoking as soon as the treatments started, but by then it didn't really matter. There was no reason. He was no fun to be around any way you looked at it, and Jenny suddenly became interested in birds all over again, explaining to Ray where they lived and how they ate and what they did in general, and like that they were there: bluebirds, black-capped chickadees, goldfinches, robins, wrens, a catbird every now and then. Hummingbirds began to visit as soon as Jenny filled up the abandoned feeder, and a female hummingbird even flew in to the house one day, and Ray caught her in his hands against a window and released her outside. Her wings fluttered in his hands and he felt her gently insert her long beak between his fingers. It was not like holding a bird at all. It was like holding a powerless alien life, her beak a sharp, inquisitive probe.

Now Jenny was at the window, the binoculars pressed against her eyes, scanning the green woods for signs of

brighter color. Ray was on the sofa trying to read a magazine article about something, but already he'd forgotten
what it was about. This happened. He was trying to enjoy it
anyway. He read a sentence about a man named Peter in a
laboratory mixing chemicals, but he didn't know why, there
was no meaning in it, no message for him. He didn't know
what the chemicals were for or who Peter was. There was a
world in every sentence, each word its own little town. He'd
discovered something important, he thought just then, but
then he forgot what it was.

"The Carolina wrens love your hair," Jenny said, still
watching with the glasses. "Most of their nest is made of it,
I think. One of them hangs there on the netting and sorts
through it, getting the best strands. The other just rips out a
beakful. I hope we find out where they're nesting."

"Just watch them," he said. "They won't go far."

She would watch them, he knew: this was what she did.
And did and did. Ever since the birds had arrived this
spring Ray had been given a good view of Jenny's back. As
a bird flew across the yard and she followed it, turning
halfway toward him, he might catch a glimpse of her ob-
scured profile—the binoculars always in the way. Still, he
could tell where her mouth was, he saw the nose quite well
and imagined what her eyes would look like if he looked
through the wrong end of the glasses she had pressed
against them: small, and very far away.

"Some male wrens will build the beginnings of nests in nine or ten different places," she says. "Then he'll take the female and show them to her, and she'll pick the one she likes the best."

"Basically what people do, you mean," he said.

Jenny turned, finally, toward him, smiling.

"You're funny, you know that?"

"I feel funny," he said, pulling the quilt up to his waist.

"Me, too," she said, not smiling, just looking.

It was cold. He pulled the quilt higher, and the magazine fell to the floor.

THE BIRDS WERE MAKING their nests out of his hair. His sister wept when he told her. Eloise was often moved to tears. She wept at the drop of a hat. And what (it occurred to him) did this really mean, *the drop of a hat*? For weeks now, he had been asking people where this expression comes from, ever since his sister cried that day, but no one knew. Keep it under your hat, that's old hat, hold on to your hat, a tip of the hat, eat your hat—he was clear on these. But he didn't get the dropping of it.

"Eloise," he told her. "I wish you wouldn't cry so much." He said, "You cry at the drop of a hat."

"I know you've always been against it," she said, between tears.

"No," he said. "Mom and Dad just never taught me how."

16

Eloise laughed a little.

"You know," she said. "I don't think I've ever seen you cry. Not even at Grandaddy's funeral, where *everybody* cried. What's wrong with you, Ray?"

She was trying to be funny, but Ray didn't laugh. He was thinking of his grandfather now, and the funeral, nearly forty years ago. It was weird, because he remembered every moment: his parents, Grammy, his grandfather's body in the little room, and how cold he was to the touch. All this he remembered, and yet he couldn't figure out where he'd left his slippers a minute before.

"You know what happened at the funeral, don't you, Eloise?" he said. "What I did in that room?"

"I know, Ray," she said. "I've always known. And you probably shouldn't have."

"I wish—"

"What?" she said, and he could hear her crying again.

"The drop of a hat," he said, and he dropped his own, hoping the illustration would help. And it did. Something happened, but he couldn't really say what it was. He was left with a mysterious understanding. He was hoping for more.

AS THE WEEKS PASSED and Jenny continued to involve herself so deeply with her birds, a strange thing began to happen to Ray: he was growing wings. He discovered them while he was soaking in his bath. No feathers yet but where his shoulder blades shaped his back like shells, a lighter bone began to stick out. He wanted to show Jenny immediately. Then he decided to wait until they were a little bit farther along. He wanted it to be a breathtaking moment. He wanted to remove his robe and have his wings fully feathered, spread wide. Then he didn't know what he'd do. Fly, maybe.

AT THE DROP OF a hat Jenny didn't cry. Jenny rarely cried. But that morning when she came into the bedroom she was crying, not sobbing the way his sister did but softly, with tears streaming down her cheeks. She was brittle and confused these days; she didn't know how to be anymore. Because this was not how she had thought things would go. They were so young, not even fifty yet, and already this life they had shared so poorly was almost over. An abrupt ending, she thought, but the beginning had been, too, and there seemed to have been hardly any middle at all. She wanted to tell Ray these things, but that morning she didn't say anything, she just showed Ray what she held in her hands: it was a little black-capped chickadee, dead, still warm to the touch.

"It's that cat," she said.

"Gotham."

"This is the third one this week. The third that I've seen. God, who knows how many I haven't."

The little bird was perfect. There wasn't a mark on it he could see. It was just dead.

"He found a nest last week," Jenny said. She'd stopped crying. She cupped the bird in her hand as though it were water. "He brought this little baby back—I watched him with the binoculars—and I ran out there and scared him so he dropped it. It was a baby thrasher, dead. Then he just turns around and gets another, then another. Meanwhile the mom and dad birds are nose-diving at him, screaming their heads off. One out of the three lived. It was the most painful thing to watch."

"Where was I?"

"Asleep."

"On the sofa."

"Yes."

"I don't remember."

"You were asleep."

"I mean I don't remember sleeping on the sofa."

"You do it all the time," she said, smiling, turning to leave with the bird. "I won't bury it. I'm just going to take him out to the woods somewhere. Set him on some pine straw. Leave him for the ants."

She went. He thought of the third this week, the babies who were killed last week, of the place she had out in the woods somewhere, a place where she set them on some pine straw, left them for the ants.

THEY PROBABLY SHOULD HAVE spoken to their neighbor before going ahead with her plan, but it was true in all the years they had lived here they'd spoken to the neighbor once, when a tree in their yard fell into his and he came out with his chainsaw to cut it up. Ray had wanted some of the wood for himself, but Morganroth said something about an ordinance governing fallen trees: since it fell in his yard, he got the wood. He was a thin man with black and greasy hair, not the kind of man you pictured with a chainsaw. It was his tree now, he said. He would use the wood for himself.

So when Jenny said she was going to put a bell on Gotham without telling Morganroth what she was up to, there was very little Ray could do but go along with her. Ray watched her from the sofa as she coaxed him to their back porch with a piece of cheese. He came easily. Gotham was not a vicious cat, he was just a vicious killer. As he ate the cheese, Jenny was able to slip the bell ring through the loop on his flea collar. Gotham shook his head, heard the bell, and began to run. He stopped, turned, jumped straight up in the air, ran again. The sound was still with him. He was still ringing: Death had a bell on, Ray thought. It was ridiculous and pathetic and painful to watch for the next few minutes, Gotham attempting to escape what essentially was a part of him now. And so Ray stopped watching. He got back in bed and picked up something to read and tried to concentrate, but what he heard was this ringing, this constant ringing for minutes, until, finally, there was silence. He got up, took another look out the window. Gotham was lying beside a tree, not moving a muscle, not even his thick black tail.

WHEN HIS WINGS CAME in he hoped they'd be bright yellow and black, like a male goldfinches'. He didn't know what determined the color of feathers, but his hair, when he had had it, was brown; he didn't know if that would matter. He'd take whatever he could get, of course, but there was no reason not to hope, even for the impossible. They were still just buds, the wings, a long way from anything glorified. He thought he should sleep on his stomach more, give them room to grow. So he slept for most of the day. And he felt lighter. When he took a deep breath he felt himself rise slightly, all of him above his bed, as in a dream.

Jenny said it was the missing hair that made him feel lighter. Ray had had a nice head of hair, thick, until the damn chemo. He always thought he'd lose it, but not like this. There was a time when he thought of his hair as part of him, of who he was. Now he was trying to think of it as expendable, his old vanity, something good for a bird's nest. His forehead beamed. Looking at himself in the mirror he thought: I am a lighthouse.

THE BELL LASTED FOR but a day: the next time they saw Gotham he was sitting a few feet from their back porch, licking one of his paws, the bell gone. The neighbor hadn't said anything to them about it. Ray saw their positions being taken now, the bird people against the cat people. When Morganroth got home this evening he'd visit, probably with his chainsaw.

Because Jenny had another bell. She'd expected this to happen, she told him, she'd expected him to remove the bell, so she bought two. And all it took was another piece of cheese to slip it on.

And now Gotham seemed to have already gotten used to the new bell already. After he finished his cheese he slinked off, ringing, to his regular place, a stump where he cleaned himself for a few minutes. Nothing happened and Ray was tired, and he was about to leave the window when Jenny stopped him: Gotham still, crouched, intent, had seen a bird. There was a dove on the birdbath. Doves were slow, the snails of the bird world, an easy mark for a cat like Gotham. But as he made his way over to him, almost crawling at first, slowly, then stepping with a cat-paw softness, the bell rang, and long before Gotham would even have had a chance the dove flew, warbling, and Gotham turned and walked back to the stump, only mildly depressed. The dove returned a few minutes later, and Gotham tried again, with the same result.

Jenny was triumphant. She even hugged Ray, she was so happy. She'd saved a life today, and who knew how many more she would save tomorrow? So she hugged Ray, and the life of the dove streamed through them. Then she let him go and picked up her binoculars, and Ray walked back to the sofa, like Gotham to his stump.

"The wrens," Jenny said. "Your hair. There they go."

RAY CALLED ELOISE AGAIN.

"Is your refrigerator running?" he asked her.

"It sure is," she said.

"That's funny," he said. "I've never seen a refrigerator running."

"Actually, mine jogs three miles a day."

It was just like when they were kids. He could close his eyes and see them by the green rotary phone in the kitchen, having a blast. Then he would come back to the present and find himself abruptly alone, on the couch in the living room, Jenny nowhere to be seen, and his chest would fill with the most terrible sense of emptiness.

"I actually called for a reason," he said.

"What's that?" Eloise said.

"To say I'm sorry."

"Oh, God."

"What?"

"This is the phone call where you say you're sorry. And I don't even know what for. But I was wondering when it was going to come."

"I *am* sorry."

"I thought you of all people might skip it," she said. "I mean, it's so Presbyterian. You get to live as dissolute and immoral a life as you want, as long as you recant at the end. And you still get to go to Heaven."

"Everybody goes to Heaven, Eloise," he said. "It's just different for everybody. I think your Heaven will probably be better than mine."

"You have a *philosophy*?"

"This surprises you?"

"A little," she said. Then, after both of them were quiet for a long time, Eloise asked him, "So what did Jenny say?"

"When?"

"When you apologized to her."

"Oh," he said, shting his legs beneath the shawl. "I haven't yet."

Eloise laughed, but it was not a happy laugh at all.

"Oh, Ray," she said. "She should have been the very first."

"Or the very last," he said.

"You've got things totally backward," she said.

"So what's new?"

"Nothing," Eloise said. "Nothing at all."

24

MORGANROTH LEFT FOR WORK late that morning, around nine-thirty, and Ray was almost asleep again when Jenny let him know it was time. She helped him up from the sofa, pulling him by both hands, then led him out the backdoor and through the thicket of small trees and underbrush separating the houses. He was gone, she said, she watched him go, but still they were walking like spies, slowing when a twig snapped, peering around corners, not talking at all. Their hearts were already racing as they took the first stairs leading to his deck, and began to beat a faster time when Gotham jumped down at them, not hissing but simply appearing. Instead of the bell, there was a little piece of paper taped to an old rabies tag. In the tiniest letters the paper said DON'T MESS WITH GOTHAM.

"Damn him," Jenny said, but Gotham gave a look as if to say he'd written it himself. Then he ran down the stairs and out into the yard.

"I think," she said, "it's over here," pointing to the edge of the deck. "That's where I've seen them go."

And sure enough, in a corner where the deck met the house there was a small opening, and as they got closer a bird, a Carolina wren, darted out of it, chirping wildly.

Jenny took the first look. On her tiptoes she peered into the opening, then motioned with her hand for Ray to look as well. The nest was made of twigs and straw in parts, Ray saw, but it was mostly him. His brown hair was woven through it into a tight concave home. There were no eggs in it yet, but there would be, he thought, he could see them there without closing his eyes, and then the tiny bald babies crying for food, and a mother, feeding them.

He could see all this happening in his hair. Jenny could, too, he guessed, she was crying. She was crying and suddenly she was holding him, convulsing, and she tried to speak but she couldn't. Words died in the fury of her tears. Finally, two words were able to escape alive, and they were what Ray expected to hear from her for a long time. Not that he wanted to, ever. But he did expect them.

"I'm sorry," she said, choking on air. "I'm sorry. I'm sorry."

"Oh," he said, "me too," though they were apologizing for two different things.

"No," she said, shaking her head. "I left you, and you got sick."

"Well," he said. "I left you first."

"Did not."

"Did too."

"Ray," she said. "You couldn't leave me. You were never really here."

But he just looked at her, as though he didn't understand.

"Hey. Let's go home," he said to her. "Let's take a nap."

"Okay," she said. "Okay."

He held her, leading her as they made their way back

26

home. He pushed the branches away from their faces, and held all the prickly ones back until she got through. As they ducked beneath the branches of the last pine tree and entered their own yard Ray stopped to take a breath, and when he did he saw Gotham no more than three feet away from the dove, ready to pounce. He had never seen a cat so close to a bird before. The bird seemed frozen to its place in the yard, and Ray couldn't imagine why it didn't fly away. Then it came to him: it was waiting for the bell. When it heard the bell the bird would fly. Ray was waiting for the bell, too. He heard it, faintly, but his wings were nothing but bones yet. He couldn't fly either. But he would, he thought. He'd do it at the drop of a hat.

Ray held Jenny's head against him, so she wouldn't see the scene unfolding before them. But he felt compelled to watch. It had taken him this long to realize that no one would be coming to his rescue, and a part of him (the part that was already dead) wondered how long it would take this dove to realize the same thing. But then the live part of Ray picked up a pinecone and threw it their way, scattering Gotham and the dove, too, one up, one out. He had saved somebody, finally, and in the aftermath he was breathless. He hadn't been sure it was possible.

FALL 1994
The Art of Love

After she came back, Ray found himself studying her, identifying the places the other man would have touched, the places he must have touched in the natural progression of their relationship.

Ray started with her face. He would have touched her face, of course, many times, and thus her cheeks, her cheeks lightly freckled as if with paprika. Her cheeks were high and round but not so high and round as to call attention to themselves, the way some cheeks or cheekbones on some woman do. Her cheeks were—Ray had actually said this to her, not long before they were married—her cheeks were like small soft pillows for her eyes, which were brown, her eyes, which had a sleepy look to them, a kind of dreaminess he had grown to love. This guy (Ray didn't like to think his name, though he knew it well enough,) probably never touched her eyes, unless it was by accident. But her eyelids he may have stroked a time or two. Ray himself had done it, so why not this other man? Her eyelids made the list. There was something strangely intimate about her eyelids, about touching them: it was like touching the white belly of a frog, the way the skin is there. In the moments just before a kiss he would have stroked her eyelids, once, maybe twice, and her eyes would have closed, and their lips—and so obviously, perhaps most obviously, he would also have to include her lips in the inventory of the places.

But it was hard to imagine this part. It was hard to imagine someone else's lips coming into direct and explicit contact with her lips, the lips of his wife. And yet this is what had happened, isn't it? It was probably the place their bodies came into contact most often, at least in the facial area, which is the area he was concentrating on now. She kissed him, he kissed her, they kissed each other. And during a long kiss, a kiss which perhaps began softly, even coyly, with their eyes briefly open, taking the other in, and then closing, as if to signal a true beginning to the festivities, he may have held her entire face in his hands. *Her entire face!* That would include the cheeks and the chin and part of the ears as well—everything but the nose.

It was conceivable to Ray that he had never touched her nose.

This was good.

Ray, being her husband, had touched her nose many times. He remembered once having said to her, "You have a—" and then reaching out with a tissue and getting it himself. The other man had assuredly never done this.

After she came back, Ray watched his wife as she absentmindedly cleaned the kitchen counters or talked to a friend on the phone, and as he did he saw the man's hands lightly touching her neck, her hair, and moving down and across her thin shoulders. "You've got my hair," she says to him in a whisper, the sound of her voice even in rebuke like a melody, their private song. Her hair is long and brown and sometimes a man's fingers can get stuck in there and inadvertently pull a strand or two from the scalp. Afterward the man may have found some of her hair circled around a finger, or hanging from one of his buttons. This had happened to Ray too many times to count; it must have happened to him as well. It was fair to say then that the man had not only touched her hair but probably had some of it still, a memento of what had once been a kind of love, some strange thing they shared, dead now—at least, that's what she said it was, dead, or over at least, whatever that meant, in so many words this is what she had said, he thought.

The rest of her was different, though, in that the rest of her, for the most part, was covered and clothed, and to touch her there a great deal more was required, a more invasive procedure, so to speak, was in order. This procedure was one Ray had been performing with her for the last seventeen years, and for most of that time had been under the impression that he was the only person in the world with that sort of access, that she was a secret she shared only with him. But the secret was out now. Now he had to look at her—as she bathed, as she dressed for work in the morning—and think of where the man had been among the secret places, and what he had done once he got there. It was a tough call for Ray because, really, where *wouldn't* he have gone? Looking at her spirited little breasts, at her ribs, which angled slightly in an arch above her stomach, and the stomach itself, which was rounded and soft and framed by her thin and delicate hips, this was territory any man would care to travel. The other man had been there. Who was Ray kidding? He'd been *everywhere*. Ray could see almost *precisely* where he had been, in fact, as if the man's fingerprints glowed in the black-lit vision of his aching heart. All of his own betrayals seemed distant now, ancient history. Hers was fresh.

And yet there was much he could not, or would not, imagine, much he chose to assume or merely skip over, the way you avert your eyes from grisly photographs in a news magazine. It was hard to think of them holding hands. But they had held hands often, Ray's wife and the man, probably in the most innocent circumstances. During the rare dinners they shared, in a car, walking back from a clandestine meeting, for a long moment as they said their final

31

good-byes: the flesh there probably sustained the longest and most enduring contact. On the very hand Ray had placed the ring, that golden ring, this man (whose name he knew but whose name he refused to repeat for fear that it had some incantatory power,) had taken it in his own.

When something like this happened, Ray thought, when a man took a married woman's hand into his own, shouldn't the man's hand suddenly fall off, or crumble into dust, or at least burn for a little while? And what about the other parts of the man's body? What about the final act ? He could not even picture it—her taking another man fully within her, sealing off every entrance and exit, claiming with this final victorious thrust her heart, her mind, her body and soul, and leaving him with the shell of someone who had the same name, the same hair, the same hands and the same eyes, wore the same ring, even, but who somehow had changed, who in some essential way was different than she was before. Though still his. His. She had come back.

Ray and his wife were together again.

AS SOON AS HE could, Ray began to cleanse her, to reclaim her, to erase from her body every last trace of the other man. Because Ray had won. The other man was gone. He had his wife, his life, back again. The other man's fingerprints, though, were all over her. Places his lips had been, his hands, and the other parts Ray couldn't bear to imagine, all these things had left their mark on her; it was Ray's job to make her his own again.

Things came slowly at first. It was impossible to resume immediately the life they'd once had. But every time he touched her was a small victory for Ray; a little bit of the man was expunged. When he took her hand in his own, it was as if he were reimprinting the touch and feel of his own hand over and through the touch and feel of the other. When he kissed her—even the cool kisses they shared at first—he was doing more than just kissing her; he was taking precedence there, on her lips. His lips were showing her lips who was boss, who truly loved her, whose lips were here when the other was gone. When he brushed a strand of stray brown hair from her eyes, when he gently took her breasts in his hands, when he brought her close to him in a hug of such needy intensity it almost hurt them both, he made her a little bit more *his* again.

Step by step, inch by inch, he brought her back home. He touched her cheeks, her chin, her shoulders, her arms and hips and legs and that place in the small of her back, that patch of filament-like hair—it took forever just to get there—but he touched that spot, too, and kissed it. He held her ears in his hands. He rubbed her toes. He wanted to climb inside her; he wished she had a pouch. Finally, one gray afternoon they made love—though in this case, the first case, it was merely intercourse. His body was having intercourse with hers, or maybe discourse. They were talking things over with their bodies. In this way he did not stray or veer from his goal until the other man was gone and he had made her his again.

But that night after they'd gone to bed he awoke—as she pulled away from him to sleep on the other side—and he realized there was a place on her he'd missed. He was sure of it. A spot somewhere in a place he didn't know about, a secret place, where he had never gone. The other man had been there, but not Ray, and Ray didn't even know where to look. Deep into the night he took inventory of his wife, until he finally fell asleep thinking, The back of her knee? A crease in her finger? The tip of her lips as they curl into a smile?

FALL 1993
After She Left Him

After she left, Ray let himself go. He didn't shave, he slept late, he drank a lot—all on the very first weekend. He unplugged the telephone and lay on his bed, or what had become his bed, the thick and lumpy futon they had stashed in the closet for company. The bed was hers and she had taken it along with the bedside table and the lamp that used to sit on the bedside table, and her books, and her chairs and the paintings and her lovely white socks. Ray spent a good part of that weekend marveling at all the empty space this created, this potential for new stuff that made him want to cry. Because he didn't want new stuff. He wanted the old stuff back.

And so he let himself go, and this process of letting himself go became his solitary source of pleasure. After his first meal alone, he burped—an act unthinkable in Jenny's presence. He stood up at the table and burped as loud as he possibly could, and the burp thundered across the silence of the house, and he was a happy man. He pictured the expression on her face, what she would have looked like had she been there hearing it. Disbelief mixed with a kind of horror and repulsion, dissolving into pity. He would have loved to see that face then, the face of his wife.

Then he farted, and that felt good in every possible way. Had she not left him, had she been there with him, he never would have experienced that gross and lovely expulsion. He would have held it back, forced it to dissipate inside his own body, where there was no telling what happened to it. But now Ray could burp and then fart, and there was no retribution. A kind of cheap thrill came with it, like static electricity. And through the low, dull ache of his sadness and regret, this was a form of hope.

From this point, it was all a wonderful downhill ride. Rumbling, noxious emissions from his orifices was just the beginning. He stopped bathing. He didn't go to work. He wore the same jeans and the same T-shirt, all week, until they became caked with his various experiences.

He had been pedaling uphill with her all this time, he told himself. Changing himself to fit her desires, becoming the kind of man he thought she had wanted—and still it didn't work. She had left him anyway.

On the fourth night, he called up a woman he knew. It was not Debbie, the woman who had been the cause of all this (she had quit her job at Ray's store and moved on, the terror of seeing Jenny two or three times a week having proved too much for her). But this woman's name was Kim. Kim . . . something. He couldn't remember her last name. Ray simply thought that she was the loneliest woman he had ever known. Lovely, too, and sweet—she often took in stray animals and nursed them back to health—but it was as if loneliness was the thing she was cut out for. She lived in an apartment building near the big mall with cats and a cockatiel who could whistle Dixie. She had long black hair and porcelain white skin, and she always seemed to be getting over some terrible cold, or some terrible man. And she liked Ray. She made this clear whenever they ran into each other, at a party or in a department store—wherever. He could tell by the way she touched his arm and stared at him without blinking for minutes at a time. She could not have been kinder or more obvious with her affection. It was as if she were planting this idea in his head: when you become as lonely as me, call.

And so he did.

HE TOOK HER OUT. They shared two whiskey sours and a Caesar salad, and a grueling conversation about organic food and the real source of AIDS, but finally they made it back to her apartment, where she willingly succumbed to his desire. Perhaps not as energetically as he could have wished, but none of this was scripted. Ray had to take what he could get.

Afterward, still in bed, Kim took Ray's hand and began to massage each individual finger, beginning from the base where it met the hand and slowly, vigorously moving upward to the end where she would tug it and her fingers would snap as they released his. She looked up to him coyly and smiled, a smile he returned. It did feel good, what she was doing. She was such a small woman that she could lie across his hips and chest and he could still breathe easily. Her bones, he thought, must be hollow, like a bird's, mostly marrow. He could hear the bird whistling in the other room.

"So is this the end?" Kim asked him.

"The end of what?"

"Your marriage," she said.

"I don't know. The beginning of the end. Maybe."

"Definitely the end of the beginning."

"Well, the middle is over and done with. I think I can say that with certainty."

They laughed.

"Do you smoke?" he asked her.

"I have some cigarettes," she said. "They may be a little stale."

"That's fine," he said, and stopped himself from asking whose they were, or how long they'd been here. She gave him one and lit it with a disposable lighter. She took his free hand and studied it, tracing the palm lines with her forefinger, her eyebrows furrowed, serious, playing the fortune-teller. He flicked the ashes into a candlestick rim.

"You will have many women," she said with a smile.

"I don't need that many," he said. "Just more than one."

He meant it as a joke, but neither of them laughed. She turned his hand over and massaged his palm.

"What's this?" she said. "A scar."

Ray resisted the impulse to jerk his hand away and hide it beneath the covers. She was prying now into his personal life.

"Every scar tells a story," she said, and rubbed the thin, straight small one with her finger. Her nail was painted red. "What does this one say?" And when he hesitated she answered. "Knife fight with street thugs? Defending the virtue of a maiden? Something like that, I hope."

She smiled. It was weird to Ray, how young she acted when he knew how old she was. It didn't seem right somehow.

"I hate to disappoint you," he said, when she wouldn't let go of his hand. "But that scar I got carving the turkey."

"Carving the turkey. Boy."

"It's a rite of passage," he said. "Every dad has to do it."

He remembered the blood pouring into the white meat, until Jenny appeared with a cloth napkin and wrapped it around his hand. James watched, amazed, as if he didn't know his dad could bleed. What a scene. It was one of those hellish holidays when no one was happy and everybody had to be unhappy together. Ray hated holidays, though, even the happy ones, but Thanksgiving he hated more than most. He didn't mind giving thanks but he wanted to do it on his own terms, when and where he felt like it, and he didn't appreciate being forced to stay home with his family, eat a turkey, watch television, and take naps. When the bleeding stopped, Jenny wrapped the finger in gauze and taped it up and insisted they go to the hospital, for stitches. But he refused. He was fine. He probably could have used a few stitches at least, though; the flesh had healed in a clumsy way. Looking at the scar now he wished he were back at that table, with his wife and his son, bleeding.

There was always somewhere else he wanted to be, somebody else he wanted to be with. Ray felt present only in the future and the past.

He put his cigarette out, looked at the ceiling, and sighed. Now what? he wondered. Kim rested her head on his chest. She pressed her ear flush against his nipple, and then moved it, little by little, left to right.

"I can't find your—wait. There it is."

"My heart," he said.

"I knew you had one. Every heart sounds different, you know." She said this as though she had listened to her share. "Each has its own sound, its own personality. Did you know that, Ray?"

"I didn't," he said, all of a sudden feeling blue. "I thought they sounded pretty much the same."

40

"You've never listened," she said.

"No," he said. "I haven't."

"Well you should."

"I will. From now on, I will."

"I mean, some sound like little drums. Some like machinery. Some not like human hearts at all, but more like the heart of some small animal. Yours," she said, and stopped, and lifted her head, thinking hard. "Yours sounds like that place at the end of a record when the needle won't lift."

And she tried to imitate the sound his heart made.

"No," she said, stopping. "It's more like this."

She tried again, stopping, starting over, again and again. And although Ray wanted to leave, had wanted to leave for some time, he stayed on a little longer, at least until she got it right.

FALL 1993
His Calluses

Jenny left as Ray was cutting the skin from the bottom of his feet with a small pair of scissors. He told her it didn't hurt, wasn't meant to, and there was no reason to leave. This skin was hard, dead, almost scaly stuff, built up over the past few months from walking, from shoes and socks and sweat and their lives together. This is where it all ends up, he told her, pointing to his foot. All the tears, the harsh words, they pool at the bottom of our bodies, and harden like wax, good for cutting. Her feet, though—this was something Ray had always noticed—were amazingly soft all over. Even the big toe, the pad beneath the big toe, while it did not achieve the degree of softness the rest of her foot did, still could only be considered soft, a softness worth the touching, very much worth the touching. And her feet were not her best part, either; she had other, better parts.

There were, for instance, her hair and her eyes and her nose and her mouth and the rest of her, on down, ending at not a bad place, a soft place, her feet, sort of orange, sort of pink. It depended on the light, or lack of it. Those were the same feet she left on while Ray cut the skin off the bottoms of his own, and, as he said to her, he told her, he did not feel a thing.

SUMMER 1992

The House He Built

It was a tree house, and it was made of one-by-twelve slats of plywood with beams running diagonally for support on the walls. It was shingled, weatherproofed, and anchored there by nothing but the tree itself, a leafy magnolia said to be more than fifty years old—considerably older than Ray—when he built the tree house in it. There was one large room where many people could be, but there was a smaller room, too, behind what Ray called a false wall. A secret room! he told his son, Jimmy, who all of this was for. The only way into the room was by lifting a set of cleverly hinged boards and crawling through the opening. Even the window in that room was disguised, so nobody on the inside or the outside would know the room existed at all. Your mother doesn't even know about that room, he told Jimmy. Not even your mother! That's how secret the room is, he said.

Since branches provided a kind of stairway to the tree house, there was no ladder, no rope. This was unfortunate, Ray told Jimmy, because it meant that there was no way to keep the unwanted from coming up. He considered for a while that maybe dropping things on the unwanted would be a good idea, but Jimmy eventually discouraged him. Somebody might get hurt, depending on what you dropped.

A password was necessary. The two of them stood at the base of the tree while Ray explained this. If you don't know the password, he was saying, you can't get in.

"We'll have to think of one," Ray said. "And it's got to be secret. Otherwise, what's the use in having it?" Jimmy looked into the branches. "Today," Ray said, "let's make the password *please*. Okay?"

"Okay," Jimmy said. "Please."

And he and Ray climbed into the tree.

There was a wicker chair in the tree house, an old mattress with splotches all over it, a portable radio. There was also an old picture of President Clinton that Ray had found in the basement. Jimmy seemed surprised to see it there.

"We're like this," Ray explained, gesturing at the picture and crossing his fingers. "We're like brothers."

Jimmy, whose mind had been on many things lately, only nodded. He hadn't asked for a tree house, he had never even thought of asking, but now he had one. It had taken his father four weeks to build it, on weekends and in the evenings after he was home from work. All this time, Jimmy had been wondering what his father had been doing in the magnolia. He had been wondering, but not enough to go out and look.

Both of them stood in the big room, Ray stooping because he was so tall.

"So," he said. "You like it?"

Jimmy nodded.

"I mean really. Do you *really* like it?"

Jimmy nodded again, a little faster this time. Still, his father seemed disappointed. His father was definitely disappointed about something.

"So what do you say?" Ray said. "Someone builds you a tree house, what do you say?"

Jimmy thought it over.

"Thank you," Ray said. "You say 'Thank you.'"

"Thank you," Jimmy said. "Thanks a lot."

RAY CAME HOME FROM work on Monday and heard music. The music was coming from the magnolia. He smiled, hurried inside and into the kitchen, where Jenny was making dinner. He was jubilant and clutched at her elbow.

"Did you see him?" he said. "Have you seen him out there?"

"What?" she said. "What happened?"

"Nothing," he said, moving away from her. "Nothing's happened. He's just up in the tree house. "Slowly, he recovered the joy he had brought in with him. "He likes it," he said. "I believe he likes it."

"You scared the life out of me," she said.

"He likes it," he said again. "He had the radio going and everything!"

"I hope he doesn't fall," she said.

"He's not going to fall," he said. "Boys that age are monkeys." He laughed. "Jimmy's a monkey."

"James," she said.

"What?"

"He wants to be called James now," she said. "He said he's ten years old and that's old enough to be called James. According to him."

"First I've heard about it," he said. He stood still for a moment, there in the kitchen, thinking. "He's not ten yet, is he?" he said. "He's not already ten?"

"No," Jenny said. "Not yet."

After taking off his tie and hanging it on a doorknob, and after taking off his coat and hanging it in the closet, he went into the bathroom and threw some water on his face, and breathed. Then he made himself a drink and walked outside. It was a cool evening in June. The radio was still on. There was music. He stood at the base of the tree and looked at the house he had built for his son. He looked at it until he finished his drink and tossed the ice into the woods behind him.

"Hey up there!" he called. "Anybody home?"

A few seconds passed before there was an answer.

"Hello?" Jimmy said.

Then the radio went off, and it was perfectly quiet.

"Dad?" Jimmy said. "Is that you?"

"It's me," Ray said. "I'm coming up!"

"Wait!" his son said, in a tone of voice his father had never heard him use before. It was a command.

"Wait for what?" Ray said. "What's going on?"

"The password," he said. "What's the password?"

"Please," Ray said, climbing. "The password is *please.*"

"No it's not." His father stopped climbing. "I changed it."

"Well what in God's name is it?" Ray said. "I can't hang here forever."

He thought for a moment he heard Jimmy laughing, or maybe it was the laughter of someone else up there.

"It's secret," his son said. "What's the use of a password if it isn't secret?"

"Come on now," Ray said. "What's the password?"

But there was no answer. He climbed to the second branch and a pinecone fell on his head.

"Jimmy!" Ray said. "I'm serious!"

"James," James said. "It's James, Dad. Didn't Mom tell you? And I've got lots and lots of pinecones."

Ray waited there a moment, wanting to go up anyway and hoping that James would change his mind. But he didn't, so Ray went back inside and made himself another drink. He sat down in his chair in the living room alone, and thought about what had happened, but thinking only made it worse. And later, when he told Jenny about it, she laughed.

"Laugh," he said. "Laugh. I *built* the goddamn thing."

THERE WAS NO MUSIC the next day, nothing, when Ray came home. In his coat and tie he climbed the branches and looked in. James wasn't there, and nothing had changed. There was the bed, the chair, Clinton. But James was missing. He was in the house, watching television. He was on the floor in the den watching television and drinking a cola, and when Ray came in, James looked at him and smiled. Then he went back to watching television.

"You're not in the tree house," Ray said.

"No," James said, briefly glancing up at him in the doorway. "I'm not."

"But I guess that's obvious," Ray said. "That you're not in the tree house, I mean. You're watching television. I guess there was no need to even mention it."

Ray walked past James, into the bedroom, and did what he did every day when he got home from work. The coat, the tie. He threw water on his face. He looked at his face in the mirror and took a breath so deep it might have been his first all day. It felt and sounded as though it was his first breath of the day. Work had been tense, lately: he'd been considering opening another store. And he had also done something he had hoped he would never do: Ray had started an affair with Debbie Martin, the woman who did his books. This afternoon, they'd actually had sex in the dim back room where she worked all alone with her calculator, in that tiny chair. Now, at home, he didn't want to think about it. Any of it. He walked back into the den where James was and sat down beside him.

After a moment he said, "I wouldn't go into that tree house either. Not if you paid me."

James didn't say anything. He was watching television.

"You know why?" Ray said. "You know why I wouldn't go up there, even if you paid me?"

He waited.

"Why?"

"No carpet," Ray said. "What a tree house needs is carpet. I don't blame you," he said. "Who wants to be in a tree house that doesn't have carpet in it? I know I don't. A friend of mine—Michael Jordan. You know Michael Jordan, don't you? Well, he and I are very close. I know him intimately, and he insists on carpet, and I don't mean just in his tree houses—of which he has several—but every-where. In fact, there came a time in his life when he refused to walk on *any* surface that wasn't carpeted. I won't be surprised if he quits playing basketball because they won't carpet the court."

"Michael Jordan?" James said.

"That's right," Ray said. "You and MJ. Two of the many people who aren't in the tree house this afternoon, who wouldn't be there even if you paid them."

James and Ray watched television together.

THE FOLLOWING SATURDAY RAY bought a roll of indoor-outdoor carpet and laid it in the tree house for his son. He was finished in less than an hour, and after he arranged the chair and the mattress to suit him, he called for James. He called and called, so loud he heard the echo of his voice come back to him—*James!*—until finally he heard the front door open, footsteps. Jenny.

She stood at the base of the magnolia and stared up at him.

"James is spending the night with Steven," she said. "What in the world is it?"

But he couldn't speak. His voice had left him entirely.

IN JULY THE DAYS were longer. It was light when Ray got home, light for most of the evening, until eight, eight-thirty, and since James had many interests, many friends, and many things to do he was rarely home, Ray never saw him. So Ray began to wait for his son in the tree house. His presence there would always surprise a bird or two—red ones, brown ones—birds he always meant to ask Jenny about, but then forgot. From the window in the tree house he could see all the way down the street toward town, where James would be coming from, probably on his bicycle or with a friend, or, if it was very late, if it was just before dark, alone, pedaling furiously, sweeping his wheels through the glass- and grass-filled gutters, trying to make it home before the light died—that is, before he would get in trouble. Ray did what he usually did—the coat, the tie, the water, the deep breath, the drink—and then, after maybe a word or two with Jenny, while she made dinner, he would climb the limbs to the tree house and wait for James there.

He was always pleased to see changes in the tree house: the carpet dirtier than it was the last time he was there, the dusty gray outline of James's shoes on the carpet, a bigger pile of pinecones in the corner, Clinton now sporting a moustache and fangs. James had been here, he had been using the tree house, and this pleased Ray. He was satisfied. The world was right. He had built a tree house for his son and his son was using it, exactly as he had planned.

He listened to the radio while he waited for James. He watched cars pass and some of his neighbors out walking, but no one saw him hidden behind the shiny green leaves and the lovely creamy white flowers of the magnolia. Debbie had the whitest skin he had ever seen. When he held her, he could see where his hands had been. What he was doing was not a bad thing, it was just a thing, something he was doing now but would eventually stop doing. He tried not to think about it when he was inside the house, but in the tree house it was okay. He thought about Debbie a lot when he was in the tree house.

When he finished his first drink he'd climb down and make another. He'd say something to his wife. Dinner was ready. She'd keep it warm.

That summer they ate at strange times or not at all, not as family, anyway, around the table. James was gone, Ray was in the tree house, and with the days as long as they were and so hot, no one seemed to have an appetite. Things would get back to normal in the fall, Ray felt sure, with James in school and the cool weather and the long nights.

Ray began to keep his bottle and a bucket of ice in the tree house. With his bottle, a glass, and a bucket of ice, he never had to move. He would be there when his son arrived. He urinated out the tree house window, feeling as though he were breaking some rule, even blushing the first time he did it, laughing to himself. He saw how far he could stream it, if he could piss past the branches and leaves all the way to the monkey grass lining the walk, and he almost made it. He was immensely pleased with himself, though it was a triumph he would never be able to tell anyone about except James, and then only when he became much, much older.

Ray never knew how drunk he was until he tried to get down. It always came as a surprise to him. Lying on the mattress, listening to the radio, he felt perfectly sober. But standing at the door to the tree house and looking at the distance between where he was and where he had to go astonished him. Was it really that far? Was the network of branches that complex? Something had changed, it seemed, while he had been resting there, so he would take off his shoes. They were not made for climbing trees. He would take them off and throw them out, then watch them fall, listening for the impact, as though he were dropping a stone down a well for the distant splash. It was not that far. Still, it was times like these Ray wished he were a bird and could jump and simply flutter down to the ground. Ray left his bottle and bucket of ice hidden beneath the pinecones. With both hands free he attempted the descent, one branch at a time. He had built this tree house, he had climbed these limbs with a mattress on his back. He knew he could do it, and he did it, and only fell once when his trousers got caught on a lower limb and tore, sending Ray on a three-foot fall, bruising his shoulder and scraping his elbow, where a small scab formed. He hadn't had a scab in years. At the office he rolled up his sleeve and worked at picking it off. Blood stains ruined a few of his shirts, and Jenny, who had to launder them, told him to stop picking at it or it would never heal. He promised to stop and did, but it took all his will, and he couldn't stop thinking about it.

Ray customarily spent the first few minutes in the tree house waiting, honestly waiting for James, but then, after a time, he forgot why he was there and began to think of other things. He thought of improvements he could make. He thought of molding, trim, paint, siding, electricity. Some personal items: a picture he liked, his button collection. He thought of an ice-maker in the corner, a small bar below the window. He would hire one of the boys in the neighborhood to serve him, or maybe one of the children of one of the black maids who took the bus here in the morning and in the afternoon. A small black child dressed in a tuxedo, mixing Ray his drinks. His name would be Charlie. His teeth would shine out from his black face, and he would not speak unless spoken to. Ray would say, "Charlie, what's going to happen to this crazy world?" And Charlie would say, "Well, sir, in my opinion, it's going to get a lot worse before it gets any better." And Ray would have to agree. "I think you're right, Charlie. I think you hit the nail on the head." A telephone, floodlights, an alarm system. A gun. He needed a gun. There'd be no fooling around with intruders, none. But girls would be welcome. Boys, too. Oh yes, girls and boys would always be welcome in the tree house, as many as could possibly fit in at one time. Debbie could come, of course, though he was noticing a weepy side she had to her that was unattractive. Still, she could come. The room wasn't big enough for all the girls he'd like to have here. Maybe only six at a time now, depending on how small they were, and the smaller the better. The younger the smaller the better. Young, teenage girls with long blond hair that had never been cut, wearing bracelets, with small round teeth, and sweet, gentle laughter.

It was very, very good to be here.

ON ONE OF THOSE rare nights, when the three of them sat down together for dinner—when James, for some reason, had nothing better to do and showed up for food, but for nothing else—his father made an announcement. Anything said around the silent table sounded like an announcement, but this one had all the force of declaration, of a new resolution. He had been in the tree house for a couple of hours, and he had been drinking. But he wasn't drunk. No, he was sure he wasn't drunk. His head was clear, and he had only come to this decision after long and careful thought.

"James," he said. "I'm sorry, but I'm taking the tree house away from you."

He was very even-toned about it, very rational. He looked at his son with his strongest eyes, eyes that were necessary for this kind of discipline. The table was silent. James's mouth was full of food, and he was trying to finish it, get it all down. He looked at his father, and then at his mother, amazed and unbelieving. Ray drew a deep breath.

"*Dear,*" Jenny said. "Ray. I'm sure you don't mean that."

"This is between James and me," he said, briefly cutting his eyes her way. "James knows what I'm talking about."

"No, I don't," he said. "I don't. It's mine."

"It was," Ray said. "It was yours. I built it for you. But I built it for you to use, for you and your friends. And you simply do not use it. You're never in it. I know, James, so don't try to tell me different."

"But Dad—"

"I'm surprised, son. I really am. I didn't think you'd mind at all. Since you're never in it, I mean. What's the use in having a tree house if you're never in it, if you don't appreciate it? So from now on I want you to consider it off-limits. I don't want you or any of your friends up there. Do you understand me?"

"*Christ,*" James said softly.

"What did you say?" Ray's fist came down hard on the table. "Repeat what you just said, James!"

"Nothing," he said.

"Did you hear him?" But his wife didn't respond. "Go to your room. Go to your room, James. Now. Without your dinner, that's right. I'll be up in a while. You and I have a few things we need to talk about."

Someone was about to cry, but then it could have been any one of the three. Finally James pushed out of his chair and stormed up the stairs, the full force of his weight on every step. His door slammed, the house shook, and then everything was quiet.

But Jenny was still there, staring. He could not send her away.

"I built a tree house for him and he never uses it," Ray said. "*Never.* He's got to learn about these things. He's almost ten years old," he said. "He's got to learn."

He looked at Jenny, waiting for her concurrence, but none came.

"Jesus," he said. "You, too."

Disgusted, he left her alone.

In the tree house, most of the ice was gone but there was still enough for a small drink. He sipped and stared out the window. The sky was purple and the clouds were orange, and it began to rain, a summer shower. Steam rose from the streets. There was a bicycle in the grass near the curb. There was thunder, lightning, and then the rain came down in sheets. Water flowed through the gutters, and the wind blew hard. Ray was pleased. Not a leak, not a drop of rain made it through the shingles. "Another one, Charlie, and make it a double." He reached for the ice bucket. "Yeah, it's been that kind of day." But he was dry. He had built a strong house.

FALL 1982
Ray in Absentia

There was a woman beside Ray when he woke up, and she was pretty. Ray really thought she was. But he was scared, and then he was worried, because he knew in his heart that he had never seen her before. He couldn't remember ever having seen her. Ray took a quick deep breath—a gasp is what it was—and the woman opened an eye and scowled at him.

"What in heaven's name is wrong with you?" she said, and she covered her ears with a pillow. "I was dreaming a good dream."

The voice surprised Ray. He couldn't think. He didn't know—for a moment it seemed to him that he knew nothing at all. He had slept for a long time, but before that? He looked over at the shape beneath the covers beside him. Who was she? What had happened last night that brought him here? He closed his eyes and thought about it, and he wondered why something like this would have to happen to him.

Ray heard the rain on the trees outside the window, dripping from the branches into puddles on the ground. It must have been raining for a long time, he thought. All night, even longer, it seemed.

"Good morning," he said to the woman.

"Morning," she said to Ray, leaving out the good.

He could see part of her face under the pillow. He looked away and shook his head. He listened to the rain and then he looked at the woman beside him again. Do the right thing, he was thinking, before you get a chance to do the wrong one again.

"Well," he said. And he laughed the way you laugh when there's no other sound you can make. "I have to tell you, this is really awful and uncomfortable for me. To say. But I can't for the life of me remember who you are. Can you believe that?" he asked her, and sort of laughed again.

She came out from under the pillow and looked at him. Then she closed her eyes and took a deep breath and let her head fall back into the bed. When finally she opened her eyes, she stared at the ceiling for a long time. He spoke again.

"I'm really sorry," he said.

She didn't say anything. Outside a car tore down the wet street.

"It's going to be another hard day, isn't it?" she said then. "You're going to make sure that today is another bad, bad day, aren't you?"

She looked at him as if she hated him and something more besides. Then she closed her eyes and turned over. Her body shook, and he thought, She's crying. This woman is crying. So they both had problems, he thought. She was his. He was sure he didn't want to know what was hers.

"Humor me," he said. He wanted to be kind, but he didn't want to be there either, both at the same time. "Take time out for a minute and humor me and tell me what happened. What your name is, and so on. I don't like the way this feels any more than you do. My name is Ray. We'll start there, how about it. My name is Ray. What's yours?"

Because the only thing Ray was certain of was that he'd never seen this woman before in the good true light of morning. He almost said that, too, but it was clear this was a very sad time he was in for. That she was sad.

Without turning over she said, "Well, I'm your wife, Ray. I'm the mother of your child. I'm the woman you swore to protect and cherish and all that—in church," she said.

What a sad woman. She came off pretty in her despair though, Ray thought, and the look fit her. He thought, She's practicing sadness. That's how she looks. She's in training to be sad.

"Ray," she said. "Try. Let's try to get through the day without this sort of thing. Jimmy being sick doesn't help I know, but we've got to pull together, don't we? We can't just give in to it."

"No," he said. He had no idea what she was talking about, but in theory—applying what she said about hope to anything—his answer would have been the same. You can't give up. Never say never, never say die. Ray didn't have a philosophy of anything, but if he did, he thought it would be that: Never give up hope. Not until the lights go out. Life was a struggle, sure, an uphill battle, but Ray was up to it. Because he was not going to quit. How could he, when there was no one on his team but him?

Ray got up and searched for his pants and slipped them on. The woman watched him. He watched her for a minute, too. She really was pretty. Her eyes looked a little swollen, but that could have been from sleep, or not enough of it, or the crying. He liked her hair, too, which was brown. He could see one of her breasts as she moved beneath the sheets, and he felt himself wanting to move toward her and touch it and he thought, Ray, you don't even know her name. She's some woman who's wishing herself into your life. He had known them, those sweet, soft but really indigent women who tried to take a night and turn it into forever. He'd known them all before, too many, too well.

The telephone rang. Both of them watched it ring for a minute.

. "Aren't you going to get it?" she asked him.

"Why?" he said. "Why should I get it? It's not for me."

"It's not for you," she said. Apparently this really amused her. "Great, Ray. That's just great how you know that. Why don't you pick up the damn phone anyway? You know. Just pick it up and say 'Hello.' As a joke. How about it?"

The telephone continued to ring. Ray began to count. Thirteen rings! Even though this wasn't his business, it made him kind of angry. He looked at the clock on the table beside the bed. It was eight o'clock in the morning. Who would call and let the phone ring so long on a morning so early? He felt sorry for the woman, somehow. He picked it up.

"Hello?" he said.

"Mr. Williams," a man said. "This is Mr. Williams, isn't it?"

"Yes," he said, feeling for a moment funny in his stomach.

"This is Mr. Williams," he said. "Who is this?"

"You know who this is, Mr. Williams," the man said in a cold voice. "After so long, I believe you know."

"This is Mr. Williams," he said again. "Who is this?"

"I don't want to waste my breath, Mr. Williams. I don't want to play games with you. We've been in touch with your employers at Stricklands. We can't give you any more breaks."

"I have no idea—"

"Time is up, Mr. Williams."

Ray told him he was sorry, but that he didn't know who he was, that while he was Mr. Williams, that was as far as it went with him.

"What do you mean?" he said. "What do you mean, that's as far as it goes?"

But he didn't know what he meant. All he could say was, "You're right about who I am."

And he hung up and looked at the woman on the bed.

"Good work, Ray," she said. She opened her eyes real wide—she almost laughed, he thought. She almost laughed at Ray. "You really told him off, didn't you?"

Before the words had left her mouth and reached his ear the telephone began to ring again.

"Who is this guy?" he said.

The telephone continued to ring, and the woman looked at Ray as though, he thought, it was his fault. But he wasn't going to answer it. Not again. He'd done that already and didn't like what had happened. "I'm sorry about this," he said. "I don't know how this person got your number. I don't know . . ." He laughed; it was the only sound he knew how to make just then. "I'm sorry."

Ray sat on the edge of the bed as the telephone continued to ring, and watched the naked woman on the far side of the bed begin to sob.

"Oh Ray," she said. "Please."

The ringing stopped. It must have rung twenty times.

It was quiet for a moment, and then the ringing began again.

"Oh Ray," she said.

She cried a little louder, and then, like a tiny echo, there was another person crying, from another room not far away, a voice crying out for its mother.

"Jimmy," she said. "Jimmy had me up all last night. Now he's up again. You slept through it. How'd you sleep through it, Ray?"

Ray shrugged and smiled, and shouldered into his shirt. He took it as a compliment. He had always been good at being able to sleep. You don't think of it as a talent until you can't do it. But he was always good at being able to sleep. He had a capacity for it.

"Listen," she said. "Ray. Check on him, would you? His medicine's on the table beside his bed. Give him a tea-spoonful, will you? Ray?"

"Yes?"

"What is it about this morning? Why are you doing this to me?"

The telephone stopped ringing, and when it did he took it off the hook. The woman didn't seem to mind. He felt it was his fault, about the phone, and so he took the responsibility, whatever that meant. He felt terrible about her. He had a memory of her; he knew they had done something. He knew they had been intimate in some way. And he hated to be the kind of man who just got up and left in the morning. In his heart he wasn't that way, but this morning he was, and to this woman he was. She would always think of him as rather ugly, and hard. It was a shame, too, he thought. Because there was so much more to him. There was so much more to him than he could show her now.

Ray told her he would check on her baby.

"A teaspoonful," he said.

She pulled the sheet and covers over her head and thanked him, and he waved, though he didn't know if she could see him beneath all that. She didn't seem to believe he was leaving. Or maybe she did, and she just didn't care. He wouldn't have, he thought, not if he were her. He would have counted his absence as a great blessing. Good things happened where Ray wasn't; it was his distance from good things, he'd come to believe, that made them happen. The farther he was from here, he thought, the faster it would all get better for her. Ray was fairly certain that this woman had fallen pretty low in her life, and that he was an example, a good example, of just how dark these times for her were. He was what happened when someone made a mistake. And who doesn't make mistakes?

He followed the small, crying voice down the plain-walled hall to a room where Snoopy and Ernie and Grover played on the ceiling above the crib. The baby pulled at his blanket with pink, curled hands; his face was red and wrinkled. He stopped crying to catch his breath and he looked at Ray, and for a moment then he seemed to stare at Ray, so that Ray almost thought his presence was going to be enough to keep the baby quiet. Then the baby took a deep breath and began to cry all over again, harder now, Ray thought, than before he had walked into the room.

Ray picked the baby up and rocked him for a minute, but the baby only got louder, his face anguished and red. How was he going to get medicine down his throat? he wondered. The noise was unbearable, too painful to go on hearing. The telephone in the bedroom started ringing again; the woman must have put it back on the hook. He could hear her crying as well, but softly, as if all the loud parts had already been taken, and the only way to be heard was with quiet, gentle sounds.

Ray was part of something much bigger than he had ever expected. The woman had a baby and here he was holding it. Jimmy. His name was Jimmy. Cute kid. His eyes were blue. He gave him his finger and he clutched it with one of his hands. And then Jimmy stopped crying so much, and Ray managed to put a spoonful of red medicine in his mouth, and set him back down in what looked like a real nice crib. He looked at him through the bars and saw how happy he seemed to be, and then how sleepy. Ray watched him struggle for a while, trying to stay in the room with all of the cartoon characters, but he just couldn't keep the sleep away, and he closed his eyes, and Ray thought that was probably the last they would see of each other.

Now there was quiet. All Ray could hear was the sound of his own feet as they moved toward the front door. He hit his pants pocket; his keys jingled. He saw the front door and quickened his step. All he had to do was open the door and close it behind him, and he would be on his way. Ray tried not to look at the living room as he passed through it, or at anything at all, for he had enough to forget about the night, and this day, and the less to forget the better. He walked with his hand outstretched toward the door.

As he grasped the knob, he felt that odd weight on his back. He turned and saw the woman staring at him. She was draped in a blanket. She had it pulled all around her. All he could see was her face. She had stopped crying. He had no idea what in the world he could say now, as he was headed out. Just because you can talk doesn't mean you always have to. So he said nothing, but gave her a nod and a smile. He opened the door and closed it behind him, and he breathed the common air, and the rain.

He drove home. He drove on the outskirts of town to avoid the early morning traffic and made it there in ten, maybe fifteen minutes, feeling tired, dirty, ready for a shower and his own good bed. He had made a mistake. He had made a mistake and he tried to forget about it. Ray parked on the street, and picked up the morning paper as he walked to the porch, and as he was looking for the key the door opened. It opened in that slow, dark way a good door has.

There was his mother.

"What a . . . surprise!" his mother said. "Ray. My good-ness. What a nice surprise this is."

She hugged him. She held him out with her arms and looked at him. She smiled and looked him over again, and then she stopped smiling. He felt his mother's hands on his arms, could smell his home behind him.

"What a nice surprise," she said again.

"Surprise?" he said, looking from one to the other. "Surprise?"

Then his mother took his hand and pulled him inside and closed the door behind him.

"Start from the beginning," she said.

She knew this was exactly what he wanted to do.

WINTER 1981

What He Saw

Ray and Jenny had argued earlier that evening, and although they went to the party together—that is, in the same car—as soon as they walked into Jim Shoemaker's living room they parted. For the next hour or so they kept the room's distance between them, moving in circles around it like a couple of lost dancers.

Ray drank a good bit. Jim Shoemaker had a lot of liquor at his parties, even before his wife left him, and he made sure everyone was being served, hopping from friend to friend with a bottle of something. He wanted everybody to get drunk, and everybody mostly did. Ray tried hard to cooperate. By nine-thirty he had to slip outside for a shot of cold air and a cigarette, just to keep his head clear and his eyes open, but even there Jim found him—"Gotcha!" he said—and forced Ray to continue, laughing as he filled his glass. He was barefooted, Ray noticed; his small white feet attracted the starlight and glowed against the dark slate of the porch.

The two men stood there for another moment, breathing audibly, and then Jim announced what a goddamn beautiful evening it was, and commented on the beautiful parts of certain women inside. He asked Ray about his wife. She was fine, Ray told him; this is good, Jim said, nodding. They resumed their observation of the night.

It had been going on for almost a year now, Jim Shoemaker's gradual entrance into the complex world of being alone, and Ray and the others had been telling themselves that they were helping him through it by coming to these parties every couple of months, meeting his new lawyers and temporary girlfriends, filling his dark and dust-filled home with laughter and their own voracious need to feel better about themselves by pitying him; that's what friends are for, Ray guessed. When the party was over they would all drive away, a herd of swerving drunks, and discuss the problem Jim Shoemaker had with drinking. The poor man, et cetera. When he was happy, you wouldn't have confused him with anybody; now he reminded you of every unhappy man you'd ever met. Maybe he needed a hobby, Ray thought, like button collecting. Things like that kept you grounded in the world.

Jim left Ray to attend to the others, and Ray tossed the drink into a shrub and walked out beyond the portico into the backyard, where he stood looking up at the winter-brilliant sky. Jim was right: it was goddamn beautiful. The stars, the spaces between the stars, even the twisted bare limbs of the tree in front of him: as beautiful as any leafy spring he'd known. Ray could see a light beaming from a neighbor's kitchen window, and a man there leaning over the sink, washing something. The window just framed him, only a few yards away past a break of small bushes. Steam rose from the sink now, clouding the window and blurring Ray's view, so he took a few steps closer. He could see this man washing a cup—a blue cup—but with his head bowed, and the steam rising, and the liquid yellow light pouring out onto the lawn, the kitchen he was in seemed sacred. He saw a woman suddenly appear from behind him and with her arms spread wide grab him by the waist and hold him tight, and he, smiling, turned. All he could see then were her arms around his back, her fingers almost meeting, and they swayed.

Ray was feeling better by then, the cold air surrounding him like a coat, shivering himself warm. He had another cigarette. He tried to remember what he and Jenny had argued about earlier, but he couldn't; only the malice he felt toward her remained. He nursed that feeling for a minute, but he couldn't keep it alive for long, and soon it vanished like his vaporized breath, and he loved her again, and wished that she were with him here, in Jim Shoemaker's backyard, looking at the stars, and the neighbors, and the iron limbs of this bare tree.

So where was she? He walked back to the house, and, unseen in the outer darkness, he peered through a living-room window and saw her. She was standing on the far side of the couch, eating a butterfly pretzel, which she held gently between two fingers, as though it were indeed a butterfly. He liked the dress she was wearing, bright red with big black buttons down the middle, the front cut just under her collarbones. He'd always loved her collarbones. She was by herself, and he wondered why no one was talking to her, when he noticed that many of the wives in the room were alone, abandoned by their husbands, either for the company of their own kind or to sift through the two magazine racks; attached to a wall, they reminded Ray of a dentist's office. Jenny was playing with some thought now, he could tell, her eyes were distant, but engaged, and then they softened, and she smiled to herself, and began to look about the room—for Ray. She was looking for Ray. This was the precise moment (he imagined) that she had forgiven him, and he was lucky enough to have caught it. In the background he saw Jim Shoemaker coming toward her with a bottle of white wine, and then stop, disappointed, as he saw her glass could not possibly be fuller. She was a delicate sipper, abstemious due to a troubled stomach, and could survive on very little, that pretzel and the wine would last her the evening. Not Jim's ideal guest, really, but he rebounded quickly. Among the dozen or so people inside, there was at least one half-empty glass to fill, and to Jim Shoemaker the glass was always half empty.

Jenny continued to nibble at her pretzel and sip her wine, unattended. Bored, he could tell, she looked at her watch and frowned and, still holding her pretzel in that hand, brought the watch up to an ear to listen. She looked at the watch again, and shook it. It had stopped. She turned a full circle, searching for a wall clock, and then began to furtively scan the wrists of the guests closest to her. Finally, she tapped Claude Mabry on the shoulder, and as he turned to her the scene shifted. Terry Nakamura stepped into his view, and so he couldn't tell what happened next with his wife, but this, in all truth, was fine, because he didn't mind looking at Terry Nakamura. She was from Japan and had that lovely light-darkness, that will to mystery, that mixture of innocence and wisdom in her features Ray found erotic in all such women. Arriving here earlier that evening, his anger and sadness still fresh, he had followed her into the bedroom; it was here, on Jim's bed, they had been instructed to place their coats. There was quite a mound there by the time Ray's topped it off, Terry's coat nestled just below. The empty arms of his camel hair mingled shyly with her blue wool, and Ray was struck by the immense certainty that this was as close as Terry Nakamura and he were ever likely to get. She had come to America six years ago to escape a marriage her parents had arranged for her, and she was still single, working as a translator for a telecommunications firm in town. In the dim light she moved quickly away from Ray and out of the room, not even looking at

74

him, as if she sensed his thoughts and their impropriety, and didn't say hello until they were both in the living room's bright and honest glare. Ray's list of Immense Certainties had hit number three: creeping baldness and a bad jump shot, now Terry Nakamura. Looking at her through the window he tried to find some flaw that would take her down a notch in his carnal estimation, and after only a few seconds of scrutiny he spotted a mustard stain on the sleeve of her blouse, and a habit she had of licking her teeth before she smiled. That was all he needed. He could now live a long life without Terry Nakamura, just as he had with all the other women who had come before her.

He heard Jim Shoemaker coming—the French doors opened with an awful creak—but by the time Jim found him, Ray had moved away from the window and back into the yard, stargazing. Jim's feet were still bare, and now the top two buttons of his rumpled yellow shirt had been undone, a telltale sign, deliberately affected, of some back room nuzzling with his new girl. Ray tried to appear interested in the sky, but there was no fooling Jim.

"I know what you've been up to, Ray," he said. He laughed and threw an arm around his shoulder. "You took a leak on my house, didn't you?"

Ray hesitated.

"You caught me," Ray said.

"Sonofabitch," Jim said, laughing even louder. "But you know what? It's not a bad idea."

Ray watched as Jim let a long steaming stream coat his nice white brick. After Jim, finished, Ray had to restrain him from going back inside and inviting the rest of the men ("And hell, I'm no chauvinist, the women, too!") to come outside and piss on the house where he had lived with the former Mrs. Shoemaker for nearly twenty years, where they had raised two children, a boy and a girl now off at college, and where every memory he had seemed to indicate by its very fullness the lean days ahead, and the lack of love or conflict, of bad tempers, of missed opportunities, imagined or otherwise. "It's why Jean didn't even want the house," he had told Ray once. "The whole place just gave her the creeps."

Me too, Ray thought, but didn't tell him: the dim light in the bedroom, the magazine racks by the mantel, Jim's ceaseless perambulations. And most of all, the way he had degenerated into this model of a broken man. It was the creeps, not Jean, that they had been trying to exorcise by coming to these parties: if they laughed enough and drank enough, they all thought, perhaps the house itself would get happy, and the awful spirit of this collapsed life would depart. But that hadn't happened yet, and it didn't seem forthcoming. So maybe Jim had the right idea after all.

RAY WAS SOBER DRIVING home later that night, and Jenny was sleepy. Her yawns were small, delicate moans. At stop signs he would take her hand and try to hold it, but then he would have to let go to shift gears, then, having shifted, attempt to retrieve it, and Ray wondered if they had given up on romance the day they bought this tiny Japanese car. Were good gas mileage and long wet kisses mutually exclusive? A big American car would break down in some picturesque locale, and as they waited to be rescued the two of them could spread out hip to hip and just do that old love thing, while this—their compact, sensible vehicle—could only take them home.

"Poor Jim," she said after a while. "He really needs help. I felt him staring at me all night, waiting for me to make a dent in my wine. He's like a vulture."

"I don't know if I would call him a vulture."

"And where were his shoes?" she asked, laughing brightly for a moment. Then she stopped and looked out the window at a darkened mall and its huge empty parking lot. "It's just becoming very tiresome," she said, "these parties." And she sighed and shook her head, as if to shake loose some thought. "Claude Mabry made a pass at me."

"He *what*?"

"I couldn't believe it—an honest to God pass. That's how old we are, you know. If we were younger I'd say he put the make on me, or made a move on me. Now they make passes."

"I guess I missed that," he said.

"You disappeared there for a while."

"I know. I needed some air."

The radio was on, but low, and hearing a song he thought he liked he turned it up and listened. But it was a different song. He glanced at her then and caught his wife's profile against the car window, and Ray could tell she was unhappy about something; this was a talent he had, the ability to recognize her darker moments. But he felt engulfed by her sadness at times like these. She had come into their marriage with expectations, while Ray had come with nothing at all; that, Ray thought, was probably their biggest problem.

She breathed in deeply, as if to sustain herself, and looked over at him.

"Aren't you even interested in what he said?"

"Of course, I'm interested."

"Well you didn't ask."

They were at a stop sign and she stared straight ahead.

"What did he say, sweetheart?"

"He wanted to know," she said, "if I ever took part in any extracurricular activities."

"No."

"I swear to God. That's exactly how he put it. Like it would look good on my resume if he—we—. He was really disgusting."

"Never one of my favorite people," he said, "Claude."

Jenny turned and looked at him, and Ray realized he had said the wrong thing, or he had omitted saying the right thing. He did both on occasion. Lights flashed across their faces as the car passed beneath street lamps, and hers, he could see, was still not a happy one. He tried to smile when he turned to her, but couldn't maintain it, and they merely exchanged their showdown stares.

"No," she said, turning away. "He was never one of mine, either."

The car felt like the small metal can it was, moving through the mostly dark and empty streets. He thought about telling her what Jim Shoemaker had done to the side of his home earlier that evening, but decided the time had already passed for such a story, and that whatever humor there was to it—and he wasn't sure how much there was—would be lost on her now. Jenny often saw the underlying poignancy of an act, where he would only see the act itself, and if they had their difficulties, and they did, he supposed they could be traced to her depth, and his lack of it. And yet even Ray sensed something special about this night. Jim's feet glowing in the starlight, the stain on Terry Nakamura's blouse, the couple in the window of the house next door: he wanted to tell her everything he saw that night, everything he knew. But she was his wife.

In the driveway, Ray turned off the lights and then the engine. Though the cold began to spread through the car almost instantly, neither of them moved to go inside. They were both too tired.

"I think I'm pregnant," she said then, her voice unchanged, unwavering.

"Really?" he said.

"I'm late," she said. "And some other things. Feelings."

"Right," he said. "Oh my gosh. Well. I mean, this is good, isn't it?"

"I think so," she said in the darkness. Ray couldn't tell where she was looking, or if she was looking at anything at all. "People just pretend to plan things like this, I think. This is the way it usually happens."

"That's probably true," he said.

Ray took her hand and held it. For a long time they sat there like that, silent, getting cold.

"So what's the plan?" he said, and she laughed. He laughed, too, and leaned over and kissed her on the mouth. This was the beginning of one thing, the end of another— he could just feel it—and when he kissed her then, it was as if for the first time, or the last. In a way it felt as if they had left time altogether and were suspended in a place between, until they were ready to resume their lives, to move ahead.

She kissed him again, and moved her face away, shivering.

"Jim's feet," she said then. "They're awfully small, aren't they?"

"Tiny. And *so* white. When we were outside—" he said, but stopped, not knowing where to begin, or where it might end if he did.

"He'll be okay, Ray," she said, touching him. "One day. More or less."

Ray thought so, too. But they agreed that in the short term he would probably catch a cold walking around like that, barefooted, in this weather, and having agreed they took themselves inside, and to bed, where they slept together, on this night and the next, and the next, and the next.

SPRING 1979
Work-in-Progress

Ray was in the living room, studying a ceiling crack, when he heard Jenny talking to herself in the kitchen. He had never taken her for someone who would talk to herself, but this was just one of the many things he had learned about her these last few years. She also loved pistachio ice cream, watched hockey games on television, and liked to fan out magazines on the coffee table as though they were a card hand. Some things he tried to understand, others he just gave up on. The talking-to-herself-thing she did he actually thought was kind of cute.

"Not again," Jenny said, her lonely voice softly echoing. "One year, okay. Two years, well, it can happen. But three? In a row?"

She could go on sometimes for minutes, as though someone were listening; maybe she knew Ray was. He wished he could hear what she said when he wasn't there, the kind of sounds she made in his absence.

He peered around the corner, to see her. She was standing in front of the sink window, her body framed in the light bristling through the pine trees. Her breasts, somewhat conical beneath her gray blouse, seemed vaguely mountainous in silhouette, rising and falling with each breath. Lately Jenny had been droning on and on about her body, how it was changing, aging, but Ray liked it better now than he ever had. There was a soft over-ripeness about it, the flesh around her hips especially, and the backs of her thighs, which had widened sufficiently to give him something to hold on to. A brief glance at them now and he felt an amorous surge. The skin around the edge of her shorts was pink; Jenny, ever the optimist, wore them tight.

He moved up behind her and gently wrapped her in his arms.

"My dear sweet Jenny," he said. "What pains you so?"

She continued to stare, shaking her head, as if, though completely encircled in his arms, the front of his body flush against the back of her own, she were still alone.

"That . . . Mrs. McCrae woman," she said, gesturing with a flip of her hand at a neighbor's house. "She got the bluebirds again."

"She *got* them?" he said, nestling his face in her neck, kissing it once. "Do you mean she's taken them hostage?

Good God. A commando raid is in order. I'll distract her while you free them. Then we'll call the authorities."

He picked up a baseball cap hanging from a chair spindle and put it on, as though gearing up for battle. Then he kissed her again.

"Ha, ha," she said, shrugging his lips away. "I put up that bluebird house our first spring here. Nothing. They checked it out a couple of times, flying around it, poking their heads in and out. But then they made their nest in *her* house. The year after that, same thing. And I just saw Mr. B take a big clump of pine straw in his beak—out of *our* yard—and fly to *her* goddamn birdhouse."

"Jenny," he said, hugging her even tighter. "Your language. And who the hell is Mr. B?"

"Mr. Bluebird," she said. "I call him Mr. B and his wife Mrs. B. They're like, a couple."

"Like us," Ray said.

She nodded, still staring.

"There is absolutely no difference between our birdhouses," she said. "I read the book. Mine is at the right height, the right side of the tree. The little hole in the house is the perfect size. Same as hers. But she gets them. Why?"

"Why?" he said, swinging her slowly from side to side. "Maybe because she's lived there longer. Maybe because bluebirds like to nest in the same house every year." Ray struggled, trying to come up with something that would serve as a complete and final explanation, so that the entire subject could be dealt with and dropped, and they could move on to other things. "Maybe because life is just not fair."

"Big help," she said, extricating herself from his hold with her arms.

"Well, I tried."

"I know," she said, touching his wrist with her fingers but still gazing out the window. "It's not that big a deal. I just can't stop thinking about it."

"I've got something here that will make you stop thinking about it," he said, moving his body into hers again, and running his palms across the slopes of her breasts.

"You're sweet," she said, turning to kiss the corner of his lips. "But I've got to pack."

"It's only an hour's drive," he said.

"I'm already late."

"Do you have to go?" he asked her. "I think I miss you already."

"You're a nut," she said. "I'll be back Sunday."

"And me without a car. How am I supposed to live?"

She laughed and walked to the refrigerator, opening it.

"Let's see. There's beer, roast beef, tomatoes, wine, mustard, beer, eggs, beer, bread and—what's that?—more beer. I think you'll be fine."

"What about extracurricular activities?" he said.

"I thought drinking beer was your extracurricular activity."

"I'll miss your wry sense of humor," he said. "And your ass."

"Make yourself useful," she said, shaking her head. "Mow the lawn."

THOUGH SHE WOULD BE away only two nights, Jenny packed a suitcase and a travel bag, which Ray dutifully carried to the car. He kissed her through the window, and she backed down the drive. When she honked, he waved, and as the car disappeared around that dangerous, hairpin curve, which made them wonder if this was the best neighborhood to raise the children they did not yet have, almost instantly Ray was lonely, not missing her so much as simply wishing he were not alone. It was Friday, almost noon, near the end of March. He had taken the day off from work, because he hadn't wanted to negotiate a ride there and back and because he was tired, and felt like he deserved it. Mr. Strickland didn't have a problem with it, of course, and Ray knew he wouldn't. Whatever Ray wanted. Mr. Strickland knew, as did Ray, that without him Strickland's would be dead by now, one of those sad, dark, and empty storefronts on a desultory street. Because Ray was gifted in retail. He was probably gifted in other ways as well, but he had calibrated his ambition to succeed where success was possible, even probable.

And now his yard loomed before him, the grass beginning to tickle his ankles, and tree limbs scattered across it from the storm the night before. He picked up the limbs he encountered on his way to the front door, and threw them in a pile just off the walkway. Then he went to the refrigerator and got a beer, his heart sneakily thumping as he drank it. Why was it that in his wife's absence he immediately felt like being bad? He never had a beer before noon, but now it seemed the right and proper thing to do, even though it was childish—especially because it was childish. He tossed the pop-top in the trash and laughed as he remembered a joke one of his customers told him while he was being fitted for a jacket.

"How many men does it take to open a beer?"

"None. It should be open by the time she brings it to you."

Jenny would not find this funny at all, which meant that he would have to tell it to her. Something else to look forward to when she got back.

The sun was bright. He found an old pair of wraparound sunglasses, and he donned them; they made him feel rakish and anonymous. He decided to skip the front yard for now and head straight to the back. The backyard was just a patch of grass yielding quickly to a stand of pine, and Ray felt he could successfully denude it of limbs more quickly, and therefore achieve that feeling of a job well done by lunch. As he bent down to pick up his first branch, he saw, almost glowing a few feet away, a bluebird. In its beak was a tuft of lint, most likely from his very own dryer: they had been having trouble with the exhaust hose. The bird regarded Ray somewhat suspiciously, then flew to a branch above him. Ray followed it. It flew again. Ray followed it. And so on. The bird—this had to be Mr. B, the brighter of the two—never let the distance between them decrease, flying from tree to tree, until Ray stopped, and watched it take the lint to the birdhouse, disappearing into the hole, and then, moments later, peering out for the all-clear, and flying away for something more. He thought of his poor wife, whose sense of betrayal was so keen that even this bird could engage it, and turned to go back home.

But he was no longer in his yard. His ornithological pursuit had taken him all the way to his neighbor's, closer to her house than he had ever been. What did Jenny say her name was? McCrae? He had seen her, many times, waving as she drove by in her white BMW; somehow, this had passed for introductions. Ray had met all his other neighbors, but her house was actually on a gravel side street, off the main one where everybody else lived. So though her yard bordered his own and he could see her house from his, it was down a long slope dotted with dogwoods—far enough away, at any rate, to forgive their lack of community spirit, a lack that seemed soon to be amended: he looked up and saw her standing at her sliding-glass doors, staring warily at the stranger wearing the sunglasses and ball cap in her yard.

Ray smiled, and waved. It was a big wave, a friendly wave. *Nothing to worry about ma'am, I won't hurt you.* He was careful not to step in her direction until she moved first. Just like the bird, he thought. She slid the glass door open, not waving but cocking her head to one side as a dog does, hearing a high-pitched, faraway sound.

"Ray Williams," Ray called out, pointing to his home, which seemed so distant now. "Your neighbor."

She shook her head, and laughed. Ray understood this to be an invitation, and he took a few steps closer.

"This is so embarrassing," she said, her voice raised to cover the distance between them. "Mistaking your neighbor for a criminal."

"Don't feel bad," Ray said, laughing, now within speaking range. "Neighbors can be criminals, too."

"Elena McCrae," she said.

Ray moved forward and took her hand, but it was cold, and he let it go. There was a moment of quiet then, as each sized the other up. She was older than Ray, but by how much he couldn't be sure. Maybe ten years. She had entered, at any rate, a later period in life, Ray's next, in which what had been so steadily, even grandly created, like a mountain, was slowly being eroded. She had a bright, if guarded smile, and tawny skin, etched with what his wife generously called laugh lines, and her yellow hair was cut in scallops to frame her face. Her eyes seemed to be blue.

"I can't believe we've never met. After three years," Ray said.

"It's awful, isn't it?" she said. "I didn't mean to be unfriendly."

"I never thought you were," Ray said.

"I'm just always going, going, going."

"Work?"

"Well, I'm a kind of professional volunteer," she said, shrugging her shoulders. "The less you get paid, the harder you have to work."

"I hear you," Ray said, trying to look beyond her for life in the house. He could spot none.

"So my apologies for not introducing myself the day you moved in."

"And mine, too. At least I've *seen* you," he said. "I've never even seen your husband."

"I hope not," she said. "He's dead."

"Oh," Ray said. "I'm sorry."

She waved her hands a bit, preempting further apology.

"May I ask what happened?"

"He had a heart attack," she said, curiously, as though the fact of it amazed her. "Four years ago." Ray stared at her. Something didn't make sense: he would have been so young, Ray thought. And Mrs. McCrae seemed to read this in his eyes. "He was thirty-seven," she said.

"A heart attack?" Ray said. "How—

"No one knows, really," she said.

"Surely they had some idea."

"There's not a medical explanation for everything," she said. "Or one that makes sense. They said some things, but in the end, really, he just had a bad heart. Defective, I mean."

"I see."

"Anyway." She smiled. "Your wife . . ."

"Alive," he said, before he could stop himself from saying it. Thankfully, she was able to laugh. "Out of town, visiting her mother."

"I've seen her, too," Elena said, and stopped there. Somehow, Ray expected her to say something like, *And a very nice-looking woman she is,* or something. But she didn't, and Ray wondered if they had had some encounter he didn't know about.

"Jenny," he said.

She nodded, not in a hurry to speak.

"Isn't this the best weather?" she asked him. "Springtime."

"Warm in the day, cool at night."

"And the birds," she said. "They're all so busy, making life."

"You like birds," Ray said, looking in her eyes now. They were definitely blue, but set so deep into her face it was hard to say without really looking.

"I love them," she said.

JENNY CALLED THAT NIGHT, as she had said she would. Her voice went from normal to a hissing whisper. So it was, "Hey, honey. How are you doing? *She is driving me stark raving mad*!"

"Your mom has that talent," he said.

"She wishes you would come more often."

"I was just there."

"For Christmas."

And so on. It amazed Ray sometimes, how precipitously their marriage had settled into a dull normalcy. Within a few months—maybe it was even weeks—they had fallen into a routine, and since then there had been little, if any, deviation from it. He had expected some interval at least when everything was magic, when merely the touch of her hand could send a shock through his system, the sight of her face gladden his heart—a honeymoon period, this was called. But even their actual honeymoon had been bleak and underwhelming. They had gone to Maine, because her mother had friends who had a cabin up there, and had found it cold and damp, even in June. Ray had had to make a fire, and Jenny laughed at him, watching him fail again and again with the wet wood, but it was a sweet laughter, the kind you expect from a wife. Still, it wasn't how he'd imagined it, his honeymoon. Nothing was how he'd imagined it.

"So," she said. "Did you finish with the yard?"

"I picked up a few sticks," he said. "Like Mr. B! But I plan to devote the whole of tomorrow to the task. When you return you will love your yard so much. You'll want to sleep in it. We'll have to move all the furniture out there because you won't want to come inside."

"I miss you," she said.

"Good," he said.

"Ray?"

"Yes?"

"When are we going to have children?"

"You mean a child."

"I want children."

"But let's do it one at a time, honey. A child first, then children."

"You didn't answer my question."

Jenny liked to save the most serious topics for phone conversations. She would call him at work and ask him if he minded her wrinkles, or if he liked it better from behind or on top, or whether it was best to be buried or cremated. She said it was the only way to talk to Ray, that at home, his eyes would wander, he would pick up a magazine, or he would simply leave the room, and Jenny would end up following him around, speaking her heart to his back. But what was he going to do on the phone? Hang up?

He opened another beer.

"I think we should do it when it feels right," he said.

"It feels right," she said.

"Hey. I'd wanted to try to make one this morning, but you—"

"*Ray*. I have to go off the pill."

"I know."

"I'm thinking about it."

"Good," he said.

"Are you thinking about it?"

"I am," he said. "I'm thinking about it."

"Good," she said.

He heard her mother's voice, from somewhere in that small, dark-paneled house, calling Jenny's name.

"*I am going insane,*" she said.

"Be strong."

"I love you, Ray," she said.

Ray said, "Me too."

ON SATURDAY MORNING HE woke up, sprawled across the bed, his mouth dry and yeasty. He had coffee, scrambled up a couple of eggs. He read through the paper, and then he watched some cartoons. Around ten, he had a beer. He felt like he was back in college. He dug out his cigarettes from a secret pack he kept in his sock drawer, and he smoked one. No matter what he said, he was probably never going to quit smoking. It was too important a vice just to give up like that.

After the second beer, picking up sticks was about all he could handle, so he wandered around, making little piles. In the backyard he heard a bright but faint good morning and looked to see Elena McCrae wave to him from her stone-slab porch. He waved back. She seemed beautiful in the distance, miniature but perfect, her strong, tanned legs slipping quietly from her shorts, her long arms, her sleeveless blouse. Her hair glowed beneath a blue bandanna.

"Beautiful, isn't it?" he yelled to her, and she nodded and resumed watering her hanging plants.

For lunch he ate an open-faced roast beef sandwich, with a beer, and went back out. Close to her lot, he saw that there were a few sticks, some weedy things with dirt-clumped roots he could pull up. She wasn't out, though, so he contented himself with thinking about her, imagining what she might be like. She was an older woman, he thought, and the very idea seemed erotic. He thought of her alternately as Elena and then as Mrs. McCrae. He wondered what her maiden name might have been. It was funny to Ray that she maintained her married name after her husband had died. Maybe everybody did it, but she was his first widow. He wondered if Jenny would do the same thing if anything happened to him, and he was torn, not knowing which to hope for. It was like being memorialized by those who had the luck to outlive you, and a big part of him hoped to be completely forgotten. So it was settled: she would be Jenny Mewborne again.

When she came out, he pretended not to see her. Perhaps, he thought, she was pretending the same thing. He bent over gathering sticks, she swept her porch. And then in the lush greenery that surrounded him he caught, out of the corner of his eye, a flash of blue, and he stood to see the bluebird, perched possessively on top of the birdhouse, a string hanging from its beak. Elena was looking, too.

LATER HE WOULD THINK it was the slim, cool wine bottle itself that was speaking to him, urging him toward his little disaster; touching it, he knew what he was going to do. It was the very ragged edge of dusk when he uncorked it, and walked with it through his yard and into hers, tripping once on a root. He knocked on her door, and waited. A minute passed and she didn't come and he was relieved, almost turning to go back, when he saw a shadow move. Then her. She squinted to make out his form, then bent to remove a stopping dowel from the base of the sliding door. He smiled throughout the entire procedure, until his face began to hurt.

"Oh," she said. "Hi, Ray. I didn't know whether I'd heard anything at first, then I thought I should check."

"This is weird," he said, "isn't it?" And he lifted the wine bottle upward slightly. "But I just thought it would be nice to share a glass, to consecrate our status as official neighbors."

"Consecrate?" she said and laughed, and he wondered if he had used the right word.

"Celebrate?"

"That's sweet," she said. "Come in." And he did.

"It's a wreck," she said, "as usual."

But there was nothing wreckish about it. There was a magazine open on the couch, and various books and papers stacked up on most every flat surface available, but Ray didn't think of this as a mess. He thought of it as a home where only one person lived. He remembered living alone. Every room was like a manifestation of his heart, or mind; the clutter without reflected the clutter within. Living with someone else masked this decorative exhibitionism. When you lived with someone else everything had to be neat, inhuman, the magazines fanned out across the coffee table, as if no one lived there at all.

"Clear off a spot and sit down," she said. "I'll get some glasses, and some crackers."

He sat down on the couch and set the wine bottle on a green triangular table. He looked around him, feeling successfully daring. There was a fireplace, darkened now, and on one end of the mantel above it a framed photo of someone who could have been none other than Mr. McCrae himself. He was on a boat, the wind blowing through his jet-black hair, looking happy, healthy. Ray couldn't help but think: Loser. You couldn't even live through your thirties. But he felt bad about the thought, briefly, until finally Elena appeared with two glasses and a tray of crackers and cheese, distracting him from it. She gave him a cloth napkin, which he placed on his lap. They exchanged smiles. Ray poured.

"I still feel awful about not introducing myself," she said. "I'm really not unfriendly."

"Timing is everything," he said. "It's funny, though, how I've seen you so much since meeting you, when I never did before. It's like when I bought my first car. It was a used Mazda 323. One of the reasons I liked it is because I'd never seen one before; I thought it was kind of rare. But right after I bought it I began seeing them *everywhere*. I parked in a garage once, and there were three of them, identical to mine, right down to the red color, in the very same row."

"So I'm like a used car?" she said, and they laughed. "Great."

"You know what I mean," he said, and she said she did. They drank his wine.

"Maybe I *am* a little unfriendly, though," she said then, as if she had given the idea some thought. "After Jim died"—and she looked at his picture—"and with him all our plans, a big family and everything, maybe I started keeping to myself. Like it was everything or nothing."

Ray nodded.

"Which, of course, is a downer," she said, rolling her eyes and brushing her hair back behind one ear. "Sorry. I'm good at bringing up sad topics."

"No," Ray said. "I feel uplifted, actually. Talking."

"I feel like a used car," she said, and then, staring intently at Ray's chest, smiled. "Are those . . . cigarettes?" she asked him.

He touched his shirt pocket.

"Oh, yeah. I didn't even know I'd brought them."

"Can we smoke one?"

"Sure," he said, and they did, knocking their ashes into the fireplace.

"I feel so wicked," she said. "This is the first cigarette I've had in weeks."

"Me, too," he said. "The wicked part, I mean."

They had another glass of wine, and another, and told each other about their lives. She was rich. After her husband died, she had poured herself into volunteer activities with the schools and the homeless shelter, just to keep herself busy, and then found that she actually liked it, darting in and out of other people's lives, making a difference, and then returning to her home. He told her, briefly, about Jenny and their life together, but it was mostly about him. He avoided the married *we*, being more comfortable with the eternal *I*.

Ray looked at her. She was beautiful, in a darkened, barren way. He found it hard to imagine there were not suitors, and he told her so, and she as much admitted that there were, but no one, yet, for whom she could trade in what she had, which was herself. Ray realized then that he wanted to be a part of her aloneness, to interrupt it, because he thought he could.

He couldn't say this, of course. But when she reached for the bottle again he reached out, too, and touched her hand, and she started, and looked at him. But she didn't move her hand.

Her lips curved into a sad smile.

"Ray," she said.

"Elena."

"No, not *Elena*," she said. "You're married."

"I was about to say the same thing to you."

Which was the wrong thing to say. She slowly removed her hand from the bottle, still looking at him, and interlocked her fingers in her lap. She breathed harshly through her nose, letting the silence separate them.

He looked away.

"I know it's wrong," he said. "I know. But it feels right. Right now, I mean."

"Well," she said, drawing herself up, "that's what we have regret for."

"Regret," he said flatly.

"You don't even know what that is, do you?"

"No," he said. "I know."

"Just not too well." She was cold, almost haughty. "Well, I suspect you'll become better acquainted with it, given time. Just not tonight."

He held the cloth napkin tight in his hand. It was time to go.

"I'm sorry," he said finally. "I just hope you'll take it as it was meant. I like you."

She smiled, but it wasn't a real smile. It was the smile of a professional volunteer.

"And I like you," she said. "We're neighbors."

BITCH. RAY DIDN'T LIKE the word but there it was. He had touched her hand, and for that he had been given a lecture on the state of his soul, from a woman he barely knew. He left hastily and wandered out into the night, standing at the edge of her porch light's glare, cloaked in darkness, surprisingly drunk, and looked back. He was, he realized, still clutching the cloth napkin. He saw her kneel, replacing the dowel. Then he saw her disappear into the other room, and then, nothing. He turned, and with small steps headed back. He stopped to get his bearings, and when he did he saw the birdhouse, barely outlined, hanging above his head. On his toes he could just peer in. He lit a match. Inside was the lint, the string, the pine straw, but no birds yet, no eggs. The nest itself was a work-in-progress. Flat-footed, he looked back at her house. Then he took the napkin, lifted himself on his toes, and jammed it into the hole, preventing any further access.

Then he walked home.

Jenny came home on Sunday, midafternoon, and she hugged Ray tight.

"*I thought I was going to die,*" she said, whispering, as though her mother could still hear her. "I am *so* glad to be home."

"And I am so glad to have you," he said, taking her bags from her and back into the house.

"The front yard looks good," she said.

"Thanks," he said. "I mowed it this morning so it would look fresh for your arrival."

"And the back?"

She walked through the living room to the kitchen, and looked out the sink window.

"Ray," she said.

"What?"

"You couldn't get to the back?"

"No," he said. "I could have."

"But you didn't."

"I didn't."

She stood, hands on her hips, and sighed.

"I could have," he went on, "but I didn't want to disturb them."

"Disturb who?"

"Look," he said.

"I'm looking."

"The birds," he said. "Mr. and Mrs. B."

"Oh. Oh my God."

And as if this were the movie version of their life together, his appearance perfectly timed, there was Mr. B,
perched proudly atop Jenny's birdhouse, blazing blue, a
long, dead vine draping from his beak. Mrs. B observed his
efforts from a distant branch. Ray and Jenny watched it all,
the edges of their bodies touching, as he flew in, flew out,
flew in, flew out, returning with a twig, then string, then a
healthy clump of lint.

Jenny stood there, transfixed, her mouth half open.

"Ray," she said. "Oh, Ray. I don't think I've ever been
so happy in my life."

"Good," he said. "That makes two of us."

He slipped his hand beneath her shirt. Then she pulled
him close, then closer, the way lovers do.

FALL 1976
The Main Thing

He simply called you, out of the blue?"

"Out of the blue," Ray said. "The phone rang and it was him. I said 'Hello?' He said—"

"And you'd never—"

"We'd never spoken before, no. Why in the world would we? Why would *he* have heard of *me*? I never knew I was heard *of,* by anyone. Not the way he is, I mean."

"But he had heard of you?"

"He called me," Ray said, and shrugged his shoulders, a gesture he thought he'd perfected. But even a shrug sometimes wasn't enough. "Not that I *am* heard of as he is. I didn't mean to imply that."

"Oh, Ray," she said, laughing. "Isn't it difficult to always be so modest? Can't you simply enjoy your moment in the spotlight?"

"I am, Jennifer," Ray told her, forcing a smile, downcast briefly by her use of the word *moment*. "But where's the spotlight?" Ray laughed. "It was just a phone call, a request."

"Well, I am very happy for you, Ray," she said, and rising on her toes as a flower stretches for the sun she planted a kiss on his right cheek. Descending, she smiled. She left no lipstick traces there, for Jennifer did not wear lipstick, but nevertheless his cheek was warm and red, flushed in a crimson glow.

"Thanks, Jennifer," he said. And then, perhaps he took a step backward where another man would have taken a step forward; he wasn't sure. Perhaps he was stepping out of the way to let somebody on the sidewalk pass. In either case, Jennifer did not seem pleased. Her face fell.

"I will be happy for me, too," Ray went on, "but for now I'm keeping my fingers crossed"—fingers he showed her—"and waiting for tomorrow. Wish me luck."

"I do, Ray," she said, regaining her normal, cheery disposition. Jennifer had a disquieting habit of saying "I do" quite a lot. Then she said it again. "I do—wish you luck, Ray."

"Good," Ray said. "And now it looks like we're late, doesn't it?" For they had met here on the street by accident, on the way to work, something they seemed to do quite often, too often, especially the past few weeks. He suspected Jennifer of lying in wait, of hiding behind city walls and storefronts, slyly creeping up on him to say good morning. But then, she managed a tea and coffee shop not a block away. It made sense that they would run into each other on occasion.

"I suppose we are," she said, not moving.

"Yes," he said.

Still she did not move.

"Well, bye then, Jennifer," Ray said, and he touched her hand with his own, just slightly, and then he walked slowly away. Feeling the fingertips of her gaze on his back he turned, and, as though she really were a flower, he watched her wave to him, a flower stirred by a breeze, still fixed to that one spot on the sidewalk while the rest of humanity spilled around her, waving. The memory of that evening—the Debacle—was still quite fresh. Memory is inescapable. So, it seemed, was Jennifer Mewborne. She disappeared as he backed still farther away, until all he could see was her hand, waving above the crowd.

BUT *HE*. THE *HE* Jennifer and Ray were talking about that morning. He was Peter Boylan, the artist. *The* Peter Boylan. Boylan was so famous that if there was a sentence with an unnamed subject in it (as in, "He simply called you, out of the blue?") Peter Boylan would in most cases rightly be guessed to be the name behind it. But that was the ironic nature of fame. One became nameless. One became so well known that introductions were redundant.

Such was the name of Peter Boylan. He was everywhere: in museums, of course, and above the fireplaces in the living rooms of the very rich, the unindicted junk-bond dealers, the financiers. But his picture was in magazines as well, on posters, his name emblazoned across sweat shirts and reproduced on the walls of cheap hotels. And yet he seemed to have maintained his dignity—or, as Ray had read somewhere, "his dignity and startling creativity."

On the other hand, Ray had heard people say that Boylan was incapable of painting a nude—this by way of criticism. And yet Ray was not one of those people who had to see a woman's breasts exposed before he'd call something a work of art. There were other things in the world to paint, weren't there? Was it always necessary to paint a breast? Ray believed the human body was beautiful. And perhaps he should leave it at that.

He managed a men's apparel store. Mr. Strickland left the day-to-day running of the store to Ray, being just over ninety years old himself and unable to see to it as he once had. A sort of music played through the store all day, as Ray measured men for shirts and slacks. Orchestrated versions of popular songs, lots of violins. This sort of music was playing when Peter Boylan called, and it was this sort of music he heard as he remembered that day. It played in the air like smoke, even then, like smoke all around him.

The store was completely empty (save for Ray) when the telephone rang. David Vickers, the young man who worked with him through the week, was off at lunch, and there were no customers at all. In a store such as Strickland's—modestly upscale, slightly pricey—there were many hours of the day when absolutely no one was there. But one good sale could make up for an otherwise quiet time. Which is to say Ray wasn't worried about there being no customers in at that moment. In the next moment he might sell a man $300 worth of trousers.

He was pricing jackets and listening to the music, to what seemed millions of violins, alone, completely unconcerned. And the telephone rang. And it was Peter Boylan. And he wanted—

A button.

He was very kind. He introduced himself as if he were just anybody, but of course Ray knew who it was: he had heard that voice on the radio before. Deep and sonorous. Reassuring. Very much there, all there.

"Mr. Williams," he said. "I'm in need of a button."

"A button?"

Ray was very close to speechless. His entire vocabulary reduced to one word.

Button.

"A button?" he said again.

"I'm sorry. Do I have the right Williams? Ray Williams?"

"This is Ray Williams," he said.

"But is this *the* Ray Williams? That Ray Williams? The one with the buttons?"

"Yes," he said, finally. "It is."

"Well. Good." He was clearly relieved. Ray heard him let out a deep breath. "I understand you have a world-class button collection."

"That's true," Ray said, loosening up a bit. "It's one of the best, I suppose. Certainly in this country. In England there might be others who—"

"I need a button, Mr. Williams," Boylan said, just like that. He sounded a bit frantic now. Obsessed, actually. He wasn't a rude man, Ray thought, but when there was something he needed, he had to have it. Perhaps Ray had read this about Boylan somewhere, he wasn't sure. But he had to have a button. "For a sort of jacket," he said and laughed. "It was a gift from my father, actually. Years ago. The buttons are apparently quite rare. You're not the first man I've called. But this must sound odd," he said, laughing. "A stranger, calling you up and wanting to look at your buttons."

"Of course not!" Ray said, too loudly. "I mean, you're hardly a stranger, Mr. Boylan. By that I mean your work of course. Is no stranger. It's quite wonderful."

"Well, thank you," Peter Boylan said. But then Ray had the feeling he was talking to somebody else, that the mouthpiece was being covered by his hand and that he was having another conversation with somebody else as he was going on and on—

"When would you like to see them?"

"I would come down today," he said, "but there are other things I have to do. And tomorrow's no good. How's Wednesday for you?"

"Wednesday is good for me, Mr. Boylan," I said.

"Peter," he said. "Please."

"Peter," Ray said, and heard the strings (it was "Yesterday," by the Beatles). "See you then, Wednesday."

A SHRUG IS AN important gesture, Ray thought, but so are the accessory gestures such as the raising of eyebrows, the dry sniffle, the studied frown, temple rubbing, the slow nod, the faraway stare, et cetera. And what are we, really, but a conglomeration of accessories, a pastiche, the sum of our scrap-bag experiences? For instance. His button collection was a direct result of his mother being unable to sew. She was frankly not that kind of mother, and his childhood was thus full of shirts perpetually worn open at the neck, or, much worse, drafty around the middle, and pants rigged with safety pins, and coats—there was never much of a problem with coats, as he recalled. And yet, from the bad comes the good. Unable to sew, his mother dropped each and every flattened orb into a soup can she kept in the cabinet beneath the sink, and, when that was full, into an old metal box once home to some perfumed powder of hers: a few of the buttons were still covered with a dusty white coat of that powder, and they were like relics to Ray, buttons saturated in her smell. And then finally, obviously it was this lack on his mother's part that led him, eventually, to become a clothier, to hem and to sew and not merely for himself, but for others, too. To become, in other words, a professional.

His mother occasionally cleaned the house top to bottom, getting rid of what she considered inessentials, and after one such cleaning gave Ray her buttons. A year or two after that he found a box of old buttons at a garage sale. Something told him to buy them, and he did, and he supposed it was actually then, almost ten years ago, that his collection began. Ray was like many people who decided to collect only after they discovered what a grand collection of things they already had. By the time he was twenty-five he had the best collection of buttons on the East Coast. There were some men (the button world is, strangely, a man's world) with a larger number of buttons to be sure, but there was only one person who had a complete set of 1931 Pearlette Stallions in their original metal casing. That person, of course, was Ray Williams.

There had been three, maybe four, newspaper articles on Ray's collection, and he could only guess that Boylan—

Peter—had seen one of these and remembered his name. The idea of Ray's name taking up space in the brain of a man of his stature was all but incomprehensible.

And so as the hours passed, steadily bringing Wednesday ever closer, though Ray continued to work, to eat, and to sleep (fitfully), other than the impending visit of Peter Boylan and his buttonless jacket, little else crossed his mind.

By MIDDAY THAT WEDNESDAY he was beside himself. Efforts to maintain his composure had succeeded superficially, but no deeper. Though he was able to serve three clients, selling one jacket, two neck ties and a pair of socks, and though he felt that if questioned later none of these three men would have guessed that anything was in the least awry, inside he was like a pot of boiling water. Each time he heard the door chimes ring his heart bubbled up and over and, feigning a friendly diligence, he would glance up to see—not Peter Boylan—but Kev Hickman, or Lou Kellison, or Ralph Garten, come to get one thing or another. Ray let David take care of them while Ray stayed behind the counter near the cash register, pretending to work on order sheets. Perhaps David guessed that something was different when he realized that after an hour with a pencil in his hand Ray had yet to write down one number.

"Something on your mind, Ray?" he asked him. But Ray smiled and shook his head and thoughtlessly began writing down orders, which would overstock the store for months. Each time the door chimes rang he knew it would have to be him, have to be, and if not this time certainly the next, and so on, until the time he was *absolutely certain* Peter Boylan had entered his store and he looked up and saw Jennifer Mewborne waltzing toward him. She smiled conspiratorially, her thick brown hair pulled back in a bun. White blouse, nicely pressed jeans. She wore perhaps a bit too much makeup, but she was perhaps older than she herself would like and therefore sought to deny the aging process as it was happening to her. She was, it seemed, turning day by day into a spinster.

"Has he come yet?" she whispered as she approached the counter. David was there as well as two customers, and they watched her. Of course, they watched her; every time a woman came into the store she was watched. Sometimes Strickland's felt like a private club for men. If ever a female entered the store it was usually a mother looking to buy a sports jacket for her son who was going to college, but that would be an older woman. Jennifer's presence was therefore rather alarming, as if some rule had been broken. And yet she was oblivious to censure.

"Jennifer," Ray said, smiling, but letting the smile die quickly. "Shouldn't you be at the shop?"

"It's dead," she said. "I put up one of those 'BACK IN 15' notes. I *love* those. Well, has he?" she asked again.

113

He looked at her, toward David and his customers, down to his order sheets.

"No," he said.

"But isn't today the day, Ray? Didn't you say—"

"Today," he said, his voice kept to church-volume levels, "is the day. He's just—"

"Nervous?" she said. She touched his hand with her own and Ray realized that his had been shaking slightly, *humming,* actually, humming like one of those beds that are supposed to relax you, but instead made Ray feel like his hotel room was directly above the train station and the 2:14 was coming through.

"I suppose I am a little nervous," he said, wishing now he had never told her about the phone call. "He *is* Peter Boylan."

"I know that, silly," she said, her hand still resting on his, which had long since stopped shaking. Her green eyes flashed. She was beautiful, in a way; Ray had to admit that. Looking at her was, at times, quite a pleasure. Ostensibly to wave at a departing customer, he removed his hand from the weight of hers, waved, then placed it out of reach behind the counter. Somehow, that was the right thing to do.

"Do you remember the first time we saw a Peter Boylan together, Ray? It occurred to me last night, as I was drifting off to sleep. Do you remember?"

Ray remembered. It was almost a year ago but Ray remembered it as yesterday: the Debacle. And frankly, the

Boylan was above the bed—a Boylan reproduction, that is—in the hotel room she rented that evening, the room with the bed, the bed with the machine on its side into which Jennifer dared him to insert a quarter, the bed in which they slept or attempted to sleep for the first, last, and only time, a desperate human error he hoped—foolishly— was forgotten and forgiven, though only a short time had passed.

"I am really busy, Jennifer," he said. "I'll tell you all about it next time I see you. So, unless you'd like to buy a pair a trousers, I think you'd better—"

But Ray's sentence was left unfinished. For at that moment he came. The door chimes rang—one high, one low, *ding, ding,* while a cello-heavy version of "Love Me Tender" wafted through the store. Peter Boylan, looking all around with an avidity, looking up and down, all around, saw Ray, finally, and smiled. Jennifer winked at Ray then and slowly backed away. As Peter Boylan approached the counter, dressed in old khaki pants and penny loafers, a faded blue denim shirt, and a kind of smocky lightweight jacket, Ray had a thought of removing himself from behind the counter—to greet him fully, as it were, perhaps a bit more warmly than he had greeted, for instance, Jennifer. But he found that he could not do it. He couldn't move. Ray couldn't leave the protective safety the glassed-in counter, full of cuff links and watches and tie clasps, afforded him. Perhaps Ray was frightened, and not a little apprehensive; perhaps it was merely a fear of meeting a famous man. He was, in any case, happy to have that counter between Peter Boylan and him as he came ever closer, and Ray placed the palms of his hands on the counter, as if to reassure both it and himself that he was not going anywhere.

"Ray Williams?" he said, extending a hand. "I knew it was you. Peter Boylan, Ray. And this, getting right to it, is the jacket in question."

It was the smocklike thing he was wearing. A light brown color, clearly quite old, stitched and patched in a half-dozen places, frayed around the collar and cuffs. Had it been Ray's it would have found its place in the rag bag long ago. But it belonged to one of the country's great painters, a painter who stood before him now, pointing, hangdoglike, to the spot where there was no button.

Ray couldn't help but notice that Peter Boylan was an attractive man. He was an attractive man. In person. He had a semichiseled face and dark Oriental eyes, and his hair (what was left of it) was swept rakishly back, silver as tinsel. An inch or two shy of six feet, and friendly looking in every way. The pictures Ray had seen of him in magazines did not do him justice. A good-looking man. So. Enough of that.

"The buttons, as you can see," he said, "are made of some sort of wood. I'm not sure—"

"Oak," Ray said, interrupting the man who painted *The Sienna Mural,* a man whose work was studied in universities throughout the world.

"Oak?" he said. "Really? You're sure?"

"Oh, yes," Ray said. "You can tell by the coloring. And the design on the button, the concentric circles resolving into the small heart at the center. That's a Phillip Hartley, and Hartley worked exclusively in oak."

Perhaps it was the counter between them that allowed him such a free range of expression, but Ray was bent on expressing himself, in saying what he knew, even as his heart seemed to be crawling up his throat at every word. As for Peter Boylan, he appeared quite transfixed by Ray's narrative, truly interested in this smallest of small things Ray had devoted a part of his life to knowing better than any other man.

"Phillip Hartley," he said. "I never knew buttons were made by people. This is news," he said, laughing. "This is really wonderful news."

"Isn't it?" Ray said, allowing himself a smile. For it was truly wonderful. Jennifer was on the other side of the store, pretending to study the dinner jackets; as she browsed, slowly coming closer and closer, Ray could sense her ears aching for sound. Jennifer was not as fond of his buttons as Ray would have liked, but then very few people were. He couldn't expect them to be. Ray had shown her a few hundred of his buttons, some of the rarest ones, and she had nodded, smiled at them politely. She had called them "nice." All she'd wanted to talk about was birds. Still, having her in the store at this moment calmed Ray somewhat. And this surprised him.

In stark contrast to Jennifer, Peter Boylan, Ray could tell, was intrigued. He was *deeply* interested in the idea that all buttons had not been and were not still always manufactured, but were in some instances the meticulous creation of a troubled, artistic soul. As Ray told him at the time, Phillip Hartley lived alone in a garret in Brooklyn, making his buttons for an Italian designer, paid by the piece. On one set of buttons he carved *The Last Supper,* on another a bas-relief portrait of himself as a child, a young adult, an old man. Ray told him this and his eyes, his dark eyes grew wider, and then wider. He shook his head.

"Worlds," he said. "Entire worlds exist around us and we never see them."

"And there's so much more," he said, because Phillip Hartley was merely the tip of the button iceberg. Peter Boylan nodded, staring at Ray and smiling, rather the way you would expect a painter to do. Ray felt as though he should move around to the other side of the counter, but the exit was simply too far away. He was afraid that if he left his position Peter Boylan might just leave, or worse, disappear. So he stayed where he was. Peter Boylan placed the palms of his hands on the counter, much as Ray had earlier, and leaned in rather closer to him than he was before. He had a face of the kind you associate with those who ride horses on occasion. Darkish, and well-done. But friendly all the same. He said to him, softly, "I must see your buttons."

And Ray answered in a near-whisper, "Of course."

"You wouldn't mind?"

"Mind? I would be honored. I have some of them here if you'd like—"

"No," he said, glancing at his wrist—where, oddly, there was no watch at all. "I have to be going now. An appointment I can't break, I'm afraid. But I could come back. Or better yet, if you'd like, why not bring them to my house? Could you do that?"

"I'd love to," Ray said. "When do you—"

"Tomorrow?" he said. "Too soon? Around six? One-ten Falls Avenue. The very end of the street there. Wonderful."

When Peter had left, Jennifer took his place at the counter, standing in the same spot he had, and she looked at Ray. She had touched very nearly every hanging garment in the store, feigning interest, loitering to eavesdrop. She had a serious-seeming face on as she stood there.

"You're going to his home?" she said.

She had obviously heard quite a bit, probably everything. She had those kind of ears.

"Yes," I said. "He wants to see my buttons." Ray said this rather smugly. He hadn't meant it to come out that way but once it had, there was nothing he could do about it. After she'd seen his buttons, she'd never brought them up again—though after the Debacle it would scarcely have been appropriate for her to ask after them, or to ask him about anything this personal. Her continuing presence in

119

his life, Ray thought, was actually something of a mystery. And yet Ray wasn't completely sorry. He felt this nameless tug toward her. He felt he had to show her that Peter Boylan was fascinated by his buttons, and therefore, by extension, fascinated by Ray.

"And you think it's a good idea, Ray? Going to his home?"

"I think it's a great idea, Jennifer," Ray said, astonished completely. "Why? Don't you?"

She shrugged her shoulders. Ray matched her shrug with one of his own, and threw in a raised eyebrow to heighten the effect.

"I just wish I could come," she said, smiling slightly. "Or be a fly on the wall."

"Oh, don't worry, Jennifer," and he patted her hand with his own. She was suddenly quite sad and charming. "I'll tell you everything that happens. Moment by moment."

"If you promise," she said, smiling again.

"I promise, Jennifer," he said, in a spirit of generosity. "Really, I do. Now, aren't your fifteen minutes up?"

THOUGH RAY DIDN'T SEE her, Jennifer Mewborne followed him home that evening. He felt her presence in the distance behind him. He would turn around at odd intervals and note a subtle disruption in his field of vision, but Jennifer was nowhere to be seen. Part of him wished she would show herself and walk beside him, the way a normal man and woman would. But that feeling soon passed. Among the reasons he began working at Strickland's five years ago was that the store was within walking distance of his home. With his buttons he felt as though he could have worked at any store in town, but Strickland's was convenient, and Mr. Strickland was clearly on his way out, a situation that was sure to benefit Ray. And so he was able to walk home, and Jennifer Mewborne was therefore able to follow him. Her coffee shop was just a block away from the store, situated in such a way as to have a clear view of their glass front doors, and thus it was in the mornings when he usually felt Jennifer's presence, those mornings as the streets filled with people, men with their papers tucked beneath their arms, with their rather self-important gaits, straight-ahead stares, their grim, clean-shaven faces. Suddenly Jennifer Mewborne would appear and wish him good morning; now he waited for her dark figure to jump out from behind some tree and say, "Good evening, Ray!" Giving him a heart attack. Killing him.

The night was cooler than he expected, his sweater wasn't warm enough against the steady wind that blew, and as he held himself with his arms and shivered he was reminded, quite against his will, of the Debacle in the hotel room with Jennifer. They had gone out to dinner. It was the fourth time they had done so, but it was obvious that, in some unnamable way, tonight was going to be different. There always had to be some progress from date to date, a man and a woman always get closer. At the end of each of the three previous occasions he had kissed Jennifer at her door, each kiss on each night moving slowly toward her lips, so that if they kissed that night he would actually hit them. But now his memory found itself relying on clichés such as candle-light and wine, of which there were both, and Jennifer's bold hand creeping across the white-clothed table to brush again and again against his own. Ray was not usually so shy with women. At one time, in fact, he'd been something of a Lothario. But those days were gone. He'd had a long dry spell. And something about Jennifer frightened Ray, primarily, her indefatigable interest in him.

They finished dinner, left, and walked to the car. He opened the door for her, and closed it. He walked around to the driver's side, got in. And there on the seat cushion was a key hooked to a piece of green oblong plastic with the number 214 written on it.

"What's this?" he said, picking it up to examine. "What's this doing here?"

It was a key to a hotel room not far from where they were parked; in fact, it was the hotel closest to the restaurant.

"You're a sly one, Ray," Jennifer said, moving across the vinyl to be closer to him. "What indeed?"

She squeezed his arm with her hand and the pressure felt liberating, in a way; all of a sudden his body was hot as a flame.

"I tell you, Jennifer, I don't know—"

"That's okay," she said, kissing him on the cheek. "It's a mystery, isn't it? It's like a treasure hunt, isn't it, Ray?"

"A treasure hunt? I don't understand," he said. "Jennifer, did you—"

"An adventure, Ray," she said, holding his arm with her hands. "Let's go see if the key fits."

Well, of course, it did. But by then he knew very well what was happening. It was Jennifer's doing, all of it. Their fourth date and here they were in a hotel room, sitting across from each other on the double beds, quietly staring at the objects that surrounded them. The telephone with its suggestive red light. The television bolted to the wall. The green shag carpet. The matchbook in the ashtray. And the Peter Boylan. Right above the bed. It seemed somewhat out of place—this wasn't the best hotel in the city—but there it was. A framed print. It was the one with the boy in the swimming pool—all blue, all different shades of blue. They both noticed it at the same time and smiled. But beyond that, Ray had no real idea of what to do next. He was there but he wasn't there. He was at a loss.

"Hotel rooms excite me," she said. "You?"

He shook his head.

"Not really," he said.

"Well. Perhaps this will," she said. Whereupon she stood up, came to him and sat down on the bed next to him.

She picked up his hand and placed it on her breast—well covered with blouse and bra, soft and warm. Good, in a way.

"Jennifer," he said. But she placed her hand over his mouth.

"I like you, Ray," she said. "I like you very much. This is not something I've done before. I want you to know that. But it's something I feel I have to do. You are so—reserved. So—I don't know—distant. You bring it out in me."

And events, from that point on, rolled along spiritedly, and Ray seemed to be part of them, but only somewhat, like the boy in the picture on the wall above them. They undressed. Eventually, they were both naked. Jennifer's body was different from the figure she cut in a dress; there seemed more to her when she had no clothes on. She was fuller, more lively. Her breasts and hips, her long white arms, and the slightly disturbing sight of her dark sex—it was like nothing Ray had imagined. Jennifer smiled as she lifted the covers for them both to slide under, turning off the light and embracing him, kissing him repeatedly on his cheeks and lips, and rubbing him all over with her hands. But where there was supposed to be progress there was none, none at all. In fact, his penis seemed to be shrinking. This had never happened to him before. Jennifer played with it for a while but eventually she had to concede, as Ray did, that nothing was going to happen at all.

It was then she dared him to place a quarter in the little machine. Reluctantly, Ray did so, and then got back in

bed, which began to shake, continuously. Jennifer smiled in
a kind of lusty way, Ray thought, and kissed him on his
cheek, on his lips, on his neck. And then, to put a better
light on things, or to suggest his lack of progress didn't matter, she gave him a great big hug. And the bed was shaking,
shaking.

Ray could stand it no longer. He pushed her gently
away from him, and removed the covers, carefully, so as not
to bare Jennifer as well, and he began to get dressed. He
suggested she do the same. She did. He drove her home in
silence. He could tell she kept wanting to say something,
but his silence would not allow it. Would not. For most of
the short ride she shook her head and looked out the side
window. He didn't open the door for her or walk her to her
home when they got there. He couldn't do it. He simply
said, "Good night, Jennifer, good night," which at the time
he thought would be his very last words to her, his very last.

THOUGH RAY HAD NEVER known it, Peter Boylan's
home was not far from his own, a mile perhaps, and since
there was no sign of rain or cold or inclement weather of
any kind he decided it would be good to walk it. He placed
a portion of his buttons in a carrying case and set out about
dusk, enjoying the light as it died on the horizon. With him
he had a small box full of Phillip Hartleys, of course, the design he was looking for exactly, which, though rare, hap-

pened to fall into his hands two years ago, when a former Strickland employee found them in his grandmother's attic, and gave them to Ray as a birthday present. Such miracles occurred, Ray thought: a box of Phillip Hartleys, a call from Peter Boylan. Incredible. Life can be so encouraging, on occasion.

His house was not difficult to find at all but even as Ray spotted it, he wondered if this was it: a modest little cottage, average in every way, sitting at the end of an equally average street. The grass in his yard was not as well trimmed as his neighbor's perhaps, but that was the only indication that an artist lived here. He had expected a sculpture, he supposed, or something more eccentric.

He knocked once, and the door opened rather quickly.

"Ray," he said, "come in, come in. I see you brought the buttons! Wonderful, wonderful. Make yourself comfortable, and I'll get you a drink."

The inside was a bit more like it. Dark, and sort of messy—but messy in a way that made it seem really artistic. It was a strategically messy house. The tables were covered with small antique trinkets and candlestick stands. Totems—Ray didn't know what else to call them—were everywhere as well. Some were carved with angels on them, others merely men. And there were paintings on the walls, but none of his own, Ray noticed. The overall effect was very much the one you would expect from Peter Boylan. Ray was pleased.

"I have been able to think of nothing but Phillip Hartley since we met," he said, bringing Ray something in a glass. "And you, of course."

"How nice," he said.

"That's a martini, by the way. It's all I've got. I hope it's okay."

"I'm sure it is," Ray said, sipping.

Peter was dressed much as he had been the day they first met. If Ray wasn't mistaken, he was dressed *exactly* as he had been the day he met him, right down to the shoes, which he slipped off as he sat down in a big chair. Ray chose the couch.

"I was able to locate my Phillip Hartleys," he said, breaking a short silence during which he had stared at Peter's socks. "Nothing to worry about there."

"I wasn't worried," Peter said, smiling. His face was dark but his smile was bright, the kind of smile that encouraged a smile in others. "This button has been missing for a year. I had literally been all over the world—not looking for the button, of course, but working. In Paris or Singapore I would ask about the button, and nobody could help me. And I come back here to this town where I live half the year—like a fairy tale—and find you. Maybe this *is* a fairy tale."

"Ha," Ray said, slipping his own shoes off as well. His feet were free agents, it appeared to him then, as each toed the other heel, dropping the shoes off to the floor. "Around the world," he said, which, by that time, seemed apropos of nothing.

"A lot of trouble to go through for a button," Peter said. "But my father gave me this jacket just before he died. I'm more sentimental than I'd like to be, and when it comes to him I'm impossible."

"I know," he said.

"You know?"

"I mean, I understand."

Ray told him how his mother was responsible for his buttons, and why, and how he still had shirts with little drops of her blood on them where she tried to sew. How his collection itself was in some ways a representation of her love for him, and a celebration of his childhood. He realized he had never spoken of his mother this way before.

"The symmetry of it all is sort of amazing," Peter said, thoughtfully. "How my father gave me this jacket, your mother the buttons. And we meet. As if our parents were saying 'Peter, I want you to meet Ray. Ray, Peter. Now run along and play.'"

Peter moved forward slightly from his chair, as if, like a little boy, he were about to jump up and, as he said, go play. Ray almost did, too. But he caught himself, settled back into the couch, smiling, his face becoming warm and red.

"Would you like to see my buttons, Peter?" he asked him then.

"Yes, Ray. Very much."

And as Peter leaned somewhat closer to Ray, Ray showed him his button collection.

RAY DID NOT SEE Jennifer Mewborne at the window that evening. He did not see her round, white face peering in through one of the lower panes. But he thought he did, out of the corner of his eye, and it startled him. Just as he was getting to the Phillip Hartleys he jerked his head left, her visage disappeared, and he took a deep, deep breath, shaken. The martini, as he feared it would, had gone to his head.

"Everything okay, Ray?" Peter asked him, touching him on the shoulder, and letting his hand rest there, but briefly.

"No, I'm fine," he said, feeling the soft pressure of his hand and rather liking it. "I thought — but it was nothing."

"Would you like another martini?"

"It's probably not a good idea," Ray said.

"So is that a yes or a no?"

"Please," Ray said, handing Peter his glass.

As Peter left the room Ray stole another look at the window: no Jennifer Mewborne. Some trick of the light, he supposed. That, or the work of his mind, to illustrate how clearly different she was from the man he was now speaking with, and how different he was with him than he had been with her. Though Jennifer and Ray had known each other for almost two years now, it was really, Ray thought, only incidentally, the way one knows the name of a street one passes frequently. He had been attracted to her, of course. And why not? She was an attractive woman. He had even wondered if something might happen, one day, between them. But then they had begun their "dating," which led, eventually, to the Debacle. It simply wasn't meant to be. They knew their parts and they played them: here I am a man, you are a woman. Here we are eating dinner. We talk and laugh and become intimate, leading to some preordained debacle. Ray didn't feel as if he was really a part of such "dates." But he *acted* as though he was, because—well, one does, doesn't one?

Tonight he felt no need to act. Though he had known Peter Boylan for less than a day he felt as though he had known him a lifetime. He was at ease with him in a way he never was with Jennifer. He was an artist, he was a man. *He liked Ray's buttons.*

"To Phillip Hartley," Peter said as he handed Ray his drink. "And to all the Phillip Hartleys everywhere."

"Yes, yes, a toast," Ray said.

They clinked glasses and drank. The martini was, Ray thought, a remarkable beverage: it made him warm and cold at the same time. Two green olives rumbled at the bottom of the glass.

"Now, Peter," Ray said, feeling rather ludicrous. "Close your eyes."

Peter did so without the slightest hesitation. Ray glanced toward the window once more and, seeing nothing, took a long look at his face. Then he cleared his throat and said, "You may open your eyes."

Peter opened his eyes and saw his button resting in the palm of Ray's outstretched hand, the perfect match for his shabby jacket. Peter stared at it, clearly in awe, then shook his head, slowly reaching out to take it. He held it in his fingers and studied it, like some jewel, turning it back and forth, marveling at its form and beauty. He placed the button against the spot on his jacket and held it there.

"This—this is a dream come true, Ray," he said, and Ray knew just then he was thinking of his father, and that he was just about to cry.

"Now all we have to do is get it on there," Ray said, trying to maintain the lighter vein.

"Perhaps you can have someone at Strickland's sew it on nicely—tomorrow? Or the next day, whenever you get a chance . . . "

"Nonsense!" Ray exclaimed, standing as well as he could under the circumstances, half drunk and shoeless. "I will do it myself, and I will do it right now!"

"No, Ray, please—"

"I insist," Ray said. "I have a needle and thread here, somewhere," he said, fishing them out of his pocket. "Ah, yes. Here it is. Now all I need is a well-lighted place . . . " Because the room they were in was rather dim.

"If you insist," Peter said, standing and leading him to what appeared to be a breakfast nook. There was a small square oak table, two chairs, and a large red lamp hanging above it all, which he turned on.

"Good enough?"

"Wonderful," Ray said, settling in. Peter sat beside him in the nook so close their knees brushed, and brushed again: what a small table this is, Ray thought more than once.

"You know this isn't necessary," Peter said, watching Ray work.

"I want to," Ray said. "I like sewing. It's so meditative, for me. I'll tell you this," Ray said, his voice dropping to a whisper. "I've been known to actually take the buttons off my own shirts, rip them right off, so that I might have a button to sew when I get the urge. On a lonely night."

"And you have the urge now?"

"I do," he said, looking up at him, and going about his work. But too eagerly perhaps: as he was bringing the needle upward he stabbed his ring finger rather severely, and just that quickly saw a thin stream of blood roll from the tiny opening he had made, only to be soaked up by Peter Boylan's jacket. A large splotch of red spread across the vacancy where the button should by now have been.

"Peter," he said. "Your jacket . . ."

Watching with horror, Ray expected anger, or at the very least sadness, indignation—whatever would be proper when a drunken tailor bleeds on a man's favorite thing in the world.

"My *jacket*?" Peter said. "Your finger! Let me see your finger!"

Ray held his finger before him. Peter took Ray's hand in his. Behind him there was a box of tissues, and he took one of these and wiped off the blood. It had dripped down to the base of his finger and pooled a bit there; in other places it was already drying. Peter wiped off what he could, but the blood kept coming, slow but steady.

"There's only one way to make this better," he said, and before he did it Ray knew what that way was, knew what he was doing even before Peter brought Ray's finger to his lips and kissed it. He was very kind, Ray thought, very kind. It was very much what a mother would do. But at the same time he realized, No: he is not my mother, and this can't be. Blood moved through his body, Ray felt it, it flowed through his body and out the little hole in his finger to Peter's mouth. Ray felt it as it moved. And on this occasion there was progress, progress where he would not have liked there to have been any, any at all, then. But some things one just can't control, and this, Ray supposed, was the main thing.

Ray took his finger from Peter's mouth and hand, and stood. Peter seemed slightly paralyzed. His eyes remained wide, his mouth rounded, his hand still hanging in the air.

"I have to go," Ray said, letting the button and his jacket fall to the floor as he stood. "I'm sorry, but I must."

"Let me get you—a Band-Aid," he said. "Please, Ray."

"No," Ray said. "I'm fine. I simply don't feel . . . good about this. I'm sorry if I ruined your jacket. Really and truly sorry. But perhaps the button will cover the stain."

Ray walked back into the living room and gathered his buttons. He brushed them into his case and shut it and clasped it, and, with Peter behind him, led himself to the door.

"I apologize," Peter said, "if I was too—what do you call it? *Forward*? I didn't mean to be. I was only trying to be helpful. And I didn't think you would mind."

"I didn't mind," Ray said, unable to look at him. "I didn't. That's why I'm going."

"So you don't want to talk about it? For a moment?"

"No," Ray said, shaking his head and staring at his own socks. He tried, but he could not even shrug his shoulders.

"I see," Peter said. "In that case—"

"Yes. In that case. Good-bye," Ray said. "Enjoy your Phillip Hartley. And good night."

And it was a good night, in many ways. The air was fresh and cool, the sky was clear, and the stars were sharp and white. They were everywhere above him. A small wind rustled the leaves on the trees as Ray walked, and he could smell dinnertime in the houses all around him.

But he was bleeding, still. Some blood had dripped on his shoes and pants leg, but he dared not bring the finger to his mouth—not yet. He had to get home quickly, and he began walking as fast as he could. Had somebody been watching him, he supposed he would have resembled a man in fast forward, his feet moved below him with such an unnatural swiftness.

And then he began to run. With his buttons clutched to his side he ran as he hadn't run in years. As the wind blew into his eyes they watered and stung and it was difficult to see, but ahead there was someone, the figure of a woman, coming toward him. It seemed she was waving. Ray thought of stopping—he didn't want to frighten a woman out enjoying the sweet night—but he could not, or would not, stop. He kept his pace. Even as he approached the woman and saw that it was Jennifer Mewborne, he almost went right by her. But at the last moment, he veered to the left just slightly and ran right into her, dropping his buttons in the clash, all of which scattered over the sidewalk and onto the street like little pieces of the man he was, while Ray held, for the life of him, onto the body of a woman.

"Marry me!" he cried, burying his face in her hair, and holding her tight—his Jennifer—who, like Ray, was stunned, but willing.

WINTER 1972
Cold Feet

Women, Ray thought. He considered the word as though it were a problem—*solve for* x—and stood up from the desk. He needed something to drink to help him write. In so many ways, he thought, men were easier than women. Men were less complex, less mysterious, less sensitive. For instance: he found a beer hidden behind the milk carton in his refrigerator, and finding it there actually made him happy. With women there was always *more,* and more was hard, especially for Ray. He was happy to have the beer in his hand, to be drinking it, to even think about drinking it. He doubted that a woman, any woman, could achieve the same level of satisfaction from a mere beverage.

Certainly not Mary. Mary was like a maze, full of dead ends and bad paths; the maze was probably infinite, at that. He had a suspicion that he would never understand her, or she him. And yet she constantly persisted in *trying* to understand, as if the attempt, no matter how foolhardy, was everything. Men's adventures were physical; women's adventures were emotional. Under such circumstances, shouldn't they just leave each other alone?

Ray drank. By the time the beer was gone, he felt ready to begin.

My dearest, lovely, sweet one, Mary,

The mailman brought me your letter today, along with the heating bill, and the news that I may already be a winner.

Of course, I opened your letter first thing. And I read it. And my heart broke into a million pieces. It did. That's what you wanted and that's what happened, words like tiny ice picks in my heart. I can't even think about it now. I have to sit down if I accidentally think about it. The words, Mary. The phrases. What was it? What was it you called me? "The worst person in the world." That was it. And the word hate. *You used that word a great deal. It did everything to me, that one word. I was nothing after I read that word. Nothing. I'm crushed, Mary. I'm done for. There is just enough left in me to write this letter, so please listen to me. Please.*

Listen: my heating bill for the month of January is $42.27—a fair assessment, I think. As soon as I finish this letter I'm going to write a check for that amount, but give some thought to it please, Mary, before I do: at least $14, or one-third of this bill, was spent keeping you warm and happy, baby, and no more than $1.34 was allotted to Kevin, who was also cold. See: I've worked it all out, sweetheart! That's $1.34; one dollar and thirty-four cents. Now, does that make me the worst person in the world? Does a lousy $1.34 make me the worst person in the world? Especially when you think in fractions: he was one-thirteenth of what you mean to me. We're talking the tiniest fractions when we're talking about him, whose name I guess I shouldn't have mentioned, the tiniest fractions. In other words, my love, what's missing from your letter is perspective. Just look at the numbers! They speak for themselves. The scales tip to your advantage— and in a big, big way! I'm talking heat here, Mary. I'm talking about true love.

So what is it? I know, I know. It's what you saw, isn't it? It's that image of me and that other person, isn't it? That's what you were thinking about when you wrote that letter, isn't it? Baby, I was wondering—could you, maybe, learn to block that? Think of the mind as a blackboard and erase? I have, for the most part. I have almost entirely forgotten that incident and only recall it now for the purposes of this letter. Who was he? What was his name? Already I've forgotten.

What I can't forget, what I'll never forget is your face the moment I saw it, the moment you walked into my small room. The expression. Never. I can't describe it but to say that it was an expression pure and amazed and innocent and unbelieving. It's an expression I've seen only once before in my life, and it was a long time ago, but I haven't forgotten, *not to this day. Have I told you about this? It was when my father, looking up from the paper he was reading, saw an elephant in the garden outside our living-room window. I kid you not. An elephant, big as life right there in our garden. It had escaped from the circus and was on its way to freedom, but stopped to visit our home for a moment, this elephant, big as big could be, standing right outside the window in the garden, eyes the size of eight balls peering in at us, my father and me, one summer, Saturday afternoon. Maybe my father had expected to see—what? A blue sky? A maple? A bird on a telephone wire? He didn't see that, though. What he saw was an elephant, and what he saw gave his face the very same expression that what you saw gave yours. They are identical, Mary! And listen to this: all my father could say when he saw it, and this in a whisper—are you listening to me?—he said, "The azaleas, the azaleas." Twice, like that, in a whisper.*

The elephant was later captured, but the garden, as my father had foreseen, was in ruins.

That was serious stuff, Mary. That was serious business. Today, however, my father and I can look back at the time the elephant trampled his garden and laugh—laugh! Needless to say, it wasn't funny at the time. Let me tell you. There was nothing to laugh about then. The event had its repercussions. But now we laugh. What I'm getting at is this: I'm hoping you and I can do the same thing, either look back and laugh or not look back at all.

I know what you're thinking, Mary. You're thinking that Kevin is not an elephant, aren't you? True, true. The thought occurred to me as well, you see—we think alike. Things would be different indeed if you had found me in bed with an elephant, and my father had seen what you had, mostly naked, standing on his azaleas.

Or would they?

Oh please be patient with me, sweetest of all things, my dear, blue-eyed Mary, all I'm trying to make here is an analogy, that's all, a simple analogy for the sake of perspective. We thought the beast was going to thrust its trunk through the window—that is, my mother thought so. She was sure of it. See, I was on the floor, about three feet away from the casement, playing with a toy car, rolling it back and forth and making car sounds. My mother reports that I always liked to hang around the floorboards, near the electrical outlets, which worried her no end, she says to this day. That day I'm wearing shorts, tiny shoes, white socks, and a dirty white T-shirt. I weigh no more than a few pounds, I'm just a little guy, and cute! So cute! My father is in his BarcaLounger reading the newspaper, and my mother is in the kitchen, cooking. Remember: in a moment she'll walk into the living room, wiping her hands on a small towel, a dead smile on her face. What I want you to imagine is this: the elephant easily crashes its trunk through the living-room window. Glass shatters. He knocks over a vase of dried flowers, a table lamp—and then he sees me. Elephant Bait. Ever so gently

*the proboscis curls around my small body, lifting me up-
ward and outward, out of the living room and my mundane
childhood, safely past the jagged edge of the window and
onto his back, where I sit listening to my father mutter, over
and over again "The azaleas, the azaleas" until the elephant
and I are out of hearing distance, gone, gone far, far away,
never to be seen again . . .*

*This never happened, of course, my tender temporarily
bitter Mary, but my mother—who came into the living room
just in time to see that fantastic rump wobble away—thought
it might have. She was not a very imaginative woman, my
mother, but she imagined this. Also, she heard what my father was saying; and that look on his face, she saw that, too.
I'll tell you—and you'll have to take my word for this—she
became seriously, seriously upset. Upset that my father's first
instinct hadn't been to jump on me, to protect me from the
elephant. I was, at the time, their only child, the first, as you
know, having been a miscarriage and Eloise yet to have arrived. Hence I was quite the precious object. My mother
spoiled and adored me. I was the world to her, and when my
father didn't try to save it, her world, she became an angry
and in many ways a different woman, all in a moment.*

*Now you know Mom. She really doesn't know how to
express anger very well. She can never come right out and
say something, what she means, especially at times like these.
She's subtle, though, and can communicate large feelings in
small ways. So she burned his toast in the morning, ironed*

awkward creases in his slacks, and rearranged the kitchen cabinets so he never knew where anything was. Things like that. Never, as far as I know, did she confront him. She was not one for a confrontation. But for days, for days and days let me tell you, she wondered about the man who sat in the BarcaLounger reading the paper, rustling it, grunting occasionally at an item that caught his eye. I remember her staring at him as though she was trying to remember who he was, where he'd come from, and what, just what this man was doing in her living room. This was her husband, yes— but who was he? She did not know, Mary; the man was a stranger. I could see it in her eyes as she mulled him over in her slow and certain way. This man she married—married—*hadn't the foresight to see what could have happened, that was the problem; he was too dull to understand* consequence, *and the meaning, if merely symbolic, of an act.*

In this way, I'm afraid, I favor my father; this apple fell entirely too close to the tree. In my case, however, the worst did happen; the elephant walked away. But you, you used your key— which I don't for a moment regret giving you and which I found this morning in the gutter outside. That lock is a quiet one, isn't it? I didn't even hear you turn it, but you did, and then you walked, or, rather, bounded, in, cold, anxious for your portion of the heat, your proper third, and saw what you saw, like my father, but unlike him saying nothing. Just looking. With that look on your face. That look I will never forget.

As to what you did see, that could bear an explanation. K.—let's call this person K.—has a circulation disease. This is what he told me, Mary. This disease he inherited from his mother, who inherited it from her mother, and so on. He put it this way: his blood is thick, like honey, and in the winter it flows, well, like honey. Not very well. His blood, in other words, wasn't traveling the length of his legs, and his poor feet were white, bordering on green. The heaviest socks weren't enough to keep his toes wriggling; without blood, I don't need to tell you, the heaviest socks over the heaviest socks are no good at all. He needed stimulation. He needed to get that flow of blood moving throughout. So when you found me with his feet in my hands—and I know where we were, baby, I know—it was an act of kindness if not altruism on my part, an extension, at least, of some good will in this wintry season.

It would have been better had you found us doing something a bit more traditional, some guy thing, like arm wrestling. Maybe you think we'd already gotten to that, and possibly other things, as well. I don't know what good can come from nailing this specificity. And what you saw was an act of intimacy, yes. But I'd like to suggest here that you can- not leave me for holding K.'s feet in my hands, and neither does that make me the worst person in the world.

Think for a second.

Now, does it?

For the record, Mary, his feet do not compare with your own. They're not even in the same ballpark. I've often thought of your feet as perfect, the way your toes slant, and your fine bones, which seem to be made of ivory . . .

Ivory. I'm surprised I never mentioned the elephant to you before, since it caused quite a stir in our little town. Without a doubt it was the most significant event of my childhood. We later learned that this particular elephant had escaped and been recaptured many times before, was, in fact, a regular occurrence with this circus. But it only happened once in our little town, and the next day's headlines were fairly predictable: GENERAL MOSBY RUNS AMOK!!! *And there was General Mosby's picture, about one one-hundredth the size he was in real life. And then on page 6A, where the story was continued, there was another picture, this one of my father, standing beside his trampled azaleas. It was a grainy photo, and I still have it, I think, somewhere. In it my father is just standing there with his hands on his hips, staring at the devastation. On page 6A. "Your father is the kind of man," Mom said, "who will always appear on page 6A." And the reason his picture was in the paper at all, for the first time since his marriage, was this: ours was the only yard General Mosby chose to visit. The rest of his doomed flight took place on asphalt and concrete.*

Why our yard, I wonder? Why my father? He lived a quiet, unspectacular life making No. 2 pencils—at a factory that eventually made him rich, by the way. Why us? I've always wondered this. That elephant changed our lives, and as you read this remember that I've had nearly twenty years to think it over. What happened was that for a few days my father became a celebrity in Birmingham. All that town could talk about was the man on page 6A and General Mosby, and UPI ran the story and it was on the news—that last, thirty-second part of the news—and suddenly everybody knew about my father, the elephant, and his azaleas. Just everybody.

Meanwhile, Mother was burning his toast.

In other words, in some mysterious way, all three of us were transfigured, changed forever, by an elephant.

The real question here is, Why didn't he shield me? He loved me. My God, the man did love me. But if he did, why were his first thoughts of his garden and why—this is the bottom line—why did the event mean so much to my mother? I don't believe my father even noticed her keen displeasure—not as much as he noticed being noticed, anyway—because today, as I told you, we can look back at the elephant and laugh. You can imagine, it's a story he tells quite often, so often that my stepmother and stepbrother both know it by heart, so well that they actually believe they were there when it happened. As for my mother, I believe her attitude was rooted in the simple fact that Father did not rise to the occasion. Rarely do men in Birmingham have a chance to rise—acts of heroism are not normally required of them—but some women, my mother among them, content themselves with the thought that if the occasion did *present itself their men would surely rise, ascend, and without a moment's notice, at that.*

In a very real sense, nothing happened. The elephant stood before the window for a second, then he left. "The azaleas," Father whispered, but loud enough for Mother to hear, and suddenly, after eight years of marriage, she saw him for who he was. She found him out. He could have sealed her devotion forever simply by leaping for me, covering me with his body and tearing me, even if it was unnecessary, *out of the deadly range of General Mosby's nose, just as I feel I could have sealed yours forever if I hadn't surrendered to K.'s very cold feet. All you ask for is fidelity, a true heart, and the will not to rise to an occasion like K. That's all you have ever asked of me, and I failed. Mary, I failed.*

Yes, Ray thought. That's good.

Bear with me here, please. I have just one more thing to say. My parents were divorced. You know that. It's no secret. But do you know when *they were divorced? Do you? About ten years after General Mosby came around, with Father's garden once again in full bloom, peak condition. I was fifteen. Ten years, Mary. It took that long. Our parent's generation took commitment much more seriously than ours does, even if it meant commitment to misery and disenchantment. Which is what it was. After the General came around, Misery and Disenchantment were the special ingredients my mother used in all her meals. You could smell it, you could taste it! For ten years she stuck it out. For ten years she burned his toast. And all that time all my Episcopalian mother was waiting on was a reason good enough to put down on paper, to file without embarrassment her extreme displeasure with the pencil maker. You can guess what the reason was, Mary, can't you? I bet you can. Women. And not one woman but many over the years, an appetite fostered by the attention he received when his picture was seen on page 6A. His head swelled, I tell you, when he saw that picture, and he thought about all the other eyes who saw it, too. But before he began to stray my mother had neither the guts nor the sense of humor to mention what happened that day the circus came to town. Maybe she didn't know it herself, or maybe, in the end, the elephant had nothing to do with it at all. Maybe I'm making this whole thing up — you decide, or not, it doesn't matter anymore — only don't leave me, my angel, okay?* Do not leave me. *I'm a good guy — I really am! I'm more like my father than I ever realized, but I'm young, young enough to learn, and not the worst person in the world. It's warm here, Mary, and so very cold outside. So warm, and I don't mind the cost paying for it. I will pay this bill in its entirety and I swear, I swear K. will never happen again. He was my elephant in the garden. Do forgive me, please, please. Mary, Mary, Mary, I may already be a winner!*

No, this wouldn't do.

He threw away the letter, got himself another beer, and started from the beginning.

SPRING 1969
The Dog He Ran Over

On his way to class one morning, cutting through an unfinished subdivision to avoid a freeway bottleneck, Ray Williams ran over a dog, a small black Scottish terrier that seemed to literally come out of nowhere and end its life beneath the right front tire of his Subaru. He had been thinking of a girl when it happened. Specifically, he had been thinking of having sex with her. This morning they had almost done it, or it seemed as if they were almost going to, and then they didn't. And so in his mind he was trying to determine the exact moment when the paths diverged. What had he done? Was it something he said? If he could understand what had gone wrong maybe next time he could avoid his mistake and together they could take the other path, the path that led to the bedroom, or the couch, or the nice, comfortable chair—which is precisely when the dog appeared, and, shortly thereafter, died.

He quickly braked and pulled over, his heart racing, and searched for the carnage; the sound of the collision had been thunderous, and he expected a bloody, terrible mess. The terrier, however, was still in one surprising piece; save for the mud caked on its paws it was nearly pristine—as if, forward motion halted, it had simply flopped to one side, and might get up, if compelled to. So he kicked it. Nudged it, really, with the toe of his tennis shoe. But it didn't budge. The small black dog was dead and heavy, the way the absence of life makes all things heavy, and burdensome. He rubbed its fur once with a hand and, feeling its dwindling warmth, felt a surge of tears—for this dog and for something else, too, like the idea of a dog, or a dead dog, or dogs he had known. But a deep breath dammed the tears back.

It occurred to him then that if he and that girl had done it this morning this never would have happened: he would have been late and missed the dog. This scene of which he now found himself a part corroborated his sense of how things should have happened: doing it would have been the *right thing* to do. Not only would it have been good for him and for this girl, who had spent the night with him last night for the first time, but it would have saved this dog's life. So in a way this was her fault, or theirs together, because if they'd been together the way he wanted to be together the world would be a better place, too. And he wouldn't have to do what he had to do now.

Kneeling on the asphalt, he rotated the dog's old leather collar to reveal a tag inscribed with a phone number, an address, and, of course, a name, the dog's name—K-9. He almost laughed at the joke—*K-9*—but then he thought that probably wasn't a very original name, and then wondered why the owner hadn't put more thought into naming his dog.

Well, he thought, regarding the name, maybe they'd try harder next time. Maybe some good will come out of this after all.

The address on the collar, 2345 Wisteria Place, couldn't be far. Ray had been here once before, dodging traffic. Every street was connected to every other, and each was named after a tree or plant: Juniper Street, Azalea Way, Blackberry Court. This so-called neighborhood, or subdivision, or whatever it was, had been started almost ten months ago, and wasn't finished; formerly forest, almost every tree had been cut down to make room for the plain, white, nearly identical houses; the differences in each design—a porch here, a gabled roof there—only served to point out how similar they were in every other way. Many of the lawns had yet to yield one shoot of grass; it was just clay and dirt, and still bore the imprinted treads of the departing trucks. It was part movie set, part ghost town. Ray drove around looking for street signs and fell deeper into a sadness he realized he'd brought here with him. Not even nine o'clock yet and he'd killed something already.

Finally, he found the street and the house. White, black-shuttered, just like all the rest. There was some grass in the yard, though, a child's plastic toys, a chewed-up Frisbee: signs of life. He had been hoping nobody was home—he'd been composing in his head the note he would leave as he drove along—but there was a car in the drive, and a figure he saw through the living-room windows, moving.

It would have been a good note, too, he thought.

He took a few deep breaths, walked to the front door, and knocked.

Ray was relieved when a man appeared: he thought he'd have a better chance with a man. Men, being men, knew the code, or the same code, at least. They knew how to handle news that would devastate a woman—and which, the truth be told, actually devastated men as well. But they didn't *show* it, which made things much easier for the messenger. This is why men went bald and died young, of course, but there is a downside to everything, he supposed, and he was glad, for the first time that day, to be on the upside of anything, even if it was the upside of dying young.

"Hi," the man said.

"Hi there," said Ray, smiling, enjoying this period of relative good feeling as long as he could. He had an idea once he broke the news things might take a turn for the worse. Even if the man knew the code it wouldn't necessarily be easy. It could be quite wrenching in a quiet, teeth-grinding sort of way.

"Anyway," Ray said, "I'm afraid there was an accident. Your dog," he said quickly, because he didn't want him to think even for a moment that it was a wife or one of his kids. "I was driving down—um—Apricot Street, I think, and wow, I mean, just out of nowhere he ran right in front of my car. Like that. It all happened pretty fast."

It was the dog's fault: he wanted to come right out and say it, but he couldn't; it didn't seem right. On the other hand, he didn't want to be blamed for something he had practically nothing to do with. He wasn't even speeding. His only sin was being in the wrong place at the wrong time, and if he had had his way he wouldn't have been there at all.

"This was K-9?" the man said.

"That's right," Ray said. "A little Scotty?"

"I see," he said, nodding, and for the first time actually smiling, possibly just to put Ray at ease. He took a deep breath and opened the door a bit wider. "So? He's dead?"

"Dead," Ray said. "But it was very quick. Came out of nowhere—out of a ditch, actually, but as far as my field of vision is concerned, nowhere. I'm really sorry."

The man shrugged his shoulders. He was wearing a plain white T-shirt, which looked comfortably well-worn;

Ray could see lots of evidence of meals from the man's past scattered across it: coffee stains, grease stains, a bit of cheese around the bottom. He hadn't shaved in a couple of days, either, and his face was dark and hairy. The jeans he was wearing seemed new, but looked a bit tight. Barefooted. This was Monday morning, and he did not seem to have been nor was he intending to go anywhere. It was strange, Ray thought: you pass these houses and never think actual lives happen inside. Weird ones at that.

"As long as there was no pain," the man said. "The idea of pain really gets to me."

"Me, too," Ray said.

"So there was no movement at all? No involuntary wriggling? You know what I mean." The man shivered, just considering it.

"Nothing like that," Ray said. "I immediately stopped and got out and he was completely, you know, still. Lifeless. He's in the gutter now."

"In the gutter, over on Apricot?"

"Yeah, Apricot," Ray said.

The man covered his eyes with his hands for a moment, and rubbed them, and Ray thought when he removed them he might be going against code and crying.

"K-9!" the man said, dropping his hands, and, far from crying, let out one strong *Ha*! "Is that not the stupidest fucking name you've ever heard in your life?"

Ray laughed, too, not because he wanted to but because if the man whose dog was dead was laughing, he felt he should laugh as well. It would have been entirely inappropriate not to laugh in the face of laughter. So he laughed.

The man let the door slam behind him and walked out on the stoop, and in the full light he looked even worse. There were dark rings of a sleepy sadness around his eyes, which didn't go away at all but deepened when he laughed. It was as though he was wearing his own death mask.

"When she named it K-9, I said, 'K-9?' And she said, the way she says things like that, 'Oh, you don't get it,' and I said, 'I don't get it? What's there to get? It's stupid. Maybe there's something else you can come up with.'" The man shook his head, disgusted, and continued. "The thing about the name—in my opinion—is that it strives so hard—too hard—to be cute and original, which it isn't. Agreed?"

Ray shrugged his shoulders and raised his hands helplessly into the air.

"I really don't know," he said, although he had thought this only minutes before. But openly pronouncing unoriginal the name of the dog you just killed seemed churlish. "I couldn't say."

"No," the man said, getting a bit excited by his subject. "That's not it. The point—to me, at least—is that she wasn't naming the dog to name it, to give it an appropriate name.

She was *trying* to be clever. See? If she named it and the name happened to be clever, that's fine. But she was trying to think of a *cool* name. Something people would hear and say, 'Wow. *Cool* name.'"

The man breathed deeply and shook his head. When he resumed speaking, his voice carried the weight of a hard-earned wisdom.

"K-9 was never that dog's real name—you know, the name he brought into the world with him. That's our job, as people, to discover their real names. And she never even tried. His real name," he said, "was Andrew. Sometimes I called him Andrew or Andy or Ange like they do on *The Andy Griffith Show,* and she hated me for it. Threw something at me once, one of her poetry books. Passionate woman, that Janet. She would never throw a phone book. It would have to be a *poetry* book." He paused, seeming to relish the memory. "But he *looked* like an Andrew. I mean, that was who he was. Did you, did you see that in him?"

"Not really," Ray said. By the time Ray got to him, he was past that. He had taken his name with him.

"Not that I care that much either," the man said. "K-9, Andrew, Andrew, K-9. It was her dog. She made that totally clear. She had him before she had me. I was his step-dad, sort of. But if I so much as picked a flea off that fucking dog she'd have my ass. I kid you not."

"I see," Ray said.

And he was beginning to see. He was beginning to see that he was in the presence of a saga here. From the man's dirty clothes to his darkened face, to the emotionally charged issue of the dog's name, Ray felt himself being drawn into a family's private little universe, a place he had no real interest in going. And now he could see boxes, boxes upon boxes, stacked in the hall behind him. Something was happening here, of which K-9 was merely the tip of the iceberg.

"My name's Richard," Richard said, extending a hand. Ray took it. "Janet's the ex-wife. Or soon-to-be ex. Just so you know."

"I'm Ray."

"Okay then," Richard said, and nodded in a way meant to suggest that Ray had now heard all the facts and could come to his own conclusions. Here you've got the ex-husband, the ex-wife, the dead dog, make up your own mind. There was an element of closure to the nod, offering a brief hiatus during which Ray could have made a break for it and headed on to class. But he didn't feel as if he could just yet. He needed something else. If he was going to share this story with anybody—his girlfriend, for instance, who liked a good yarn sometimes—he needed more.

"So, cool toys," Ray said, gamely trying for a light-hearted vein, and Richard laughed, if a little bleakly. "Where are your kids?"

"No kids," he said. "These toys, they were all for the dog. We're selling the house. Lived here five months, if you

156

can call it living. A lot of these boxes back here we never even unpacked. I don't think we really held out much hope for it. Or us."

Ray kicked the dirt with the toe of his tennis shoe, uncomfortable.

"So what about K-9?"

"You mean Andrew?"

"Sure."

"She was coming by to get him today."

"*Today*?"

"She was having trouble finding a place that allowed pets, now that we're both returning to apartment dwelling. So even though she's been a bitch throughout this entire proceeding I told her I'd keep him here until she was set up, because, you know, I've got a heart as big as Texas. But this is called irony, I guess. That this should happen on the very day. Not yesterday or the day before. But today."

No, Ray was pretty sure, it's called tragedy. It's a terrible tragedy: he had studied that last semester. But he smiled and nodded anyway, backing down the red-brick stairs, relieved at the very least that he had missed this Janet: facing her would have been too hard. He looked at the toys scattered across the yard—a football, a small chair, a miniature table—and determined that there had been a child in this marriage, and it was K-9. The marriage was dead, and now the child was dead, too, and Ray had killed it.

Suddenly, he felt a surge of tears coming on again. This time, though, it wasn't merely K-9 or Richard or Janet that caused them: it was the thought of his own life. He didn't have a kid, and he didn't really want one—he was only nineteen years old—but the idea of having something like a kid really moved him. He didn't want to be like Richard and Janet, not having a child and using a dog as a stand-in— a dog that played so freely in the street, at that. His next thought of course was how awful it would be to lose a child if he did have one, but then not having one was, in a way, worse, for he would never have a chance to grieve what must be a never-ending grief, to endure the worst, as a hero endures. He was just one part of a puny two-part thing, and that didn't seem to amount to much to him today.

"She's going to be upset," Ray said, shaking his head. "Isn't she?"

Richard rubbed his face again. He rubbed it as though he were trying to rub it right off. Then he laughed. Richard seemed to laugh at all the wrong times.

"No," he said. "Actually, she's not. Janet gets upset when her coffee's a little weak. She gets upset when you accidentally take all the covers. She gets upset when you ask if for once in her fucking life she might try to be on time. With something like this—something big like this, something really, really extremely big—she won't get upset. She'll get . . . homicidal. See, she's not good at expressing herself except in a highly grandiose fashion: that's what the psychiatrist said. That means she's very theatrical. The world is her stage!"

Richard laughed again, this time louder than before. It was almost as though he were having a good time here, as though he were some lonely hermit-type who took his company where he could get it, and if it meant having to lose an ex-wife's dog as part of the bargain, well, so much the better. But Ray liked him, in a way, though *like* was perhaps too strong a word: Richard was clearly in the process of being devastated, and losing a home and a wife—which might explain the ill-timed laughter. But this is not why Ray sort of liked him: Ray liked him because he wasn't giving up. He seemed to cling tenaciously—almost absurdly—to a scrap of his life, or his former self, or something. He admired Richard, for under similar circumstances Ray imagined himself sinking, fast.

Then, from the hollow, echoing chambers inside the house, the telephone began to ring.

"Stay," Richard said, probably out of habit. "I'll be right back."

Ray thought of going, of getting in his car and leaving this scene of perpetual sadness behind forever. But the thought of one day bumping into Richard at a shopping mall or the grocery store was too terrible—he would feel like some kind of fugitive. No, it couldn't hurt to stay another minute and see if there was anything else he could do. He thought of his own dog getting run over when he was a boy, over ten years ago now: Bones, an old white mutt, killed just as K-9 had been killed. That driver didn't stop, however. It was tragic, but ironic also; Bones had been one day away from graduating from obedience school. One day away. Ray's mother, grief-stricken at watching her son endure his first death, was at a loss at how to comfort him. She cried more than Ray cried, and she gave him money. She always gave him money when bad things happened.

Richard came back to the porch, holding a black phone attached to the longest cord he'd ever seen in one hand, the other cupped over the mouthpiece.

"Ray," he said, in a semiwhisper. "She wants to talk to you."

"Who?"

"Janet," he said.

"*Janet*?" Ray shook his head, as though in shock. "I don't think so, Richard. Not a good idea. Did you tell her?"

"I told her that *something* had happened," he said, wincing, either at the thought of what had happened to K-9 or what had happened to Janet when he told her. "I didn't tell her what, exactly. But I think she's got the idea that whatever it is, it isn't good."

He held the telephone out for Ray to take, but Ray wasn't taking.

"Why do I have to get involved in this?" he whispered. "You're already getting divorced. You hate each other. Why not just go with that?"

"First of all, *Ray*," Richard said, covering the mouth-piece again, "you got involved in this when you ran over Andrew. Second, the divorce is not final, yet. And third, I do not hate my wife, and I resent the hell out of some stranger coming along, killing the dog, and telling me that I do."

Maybe Ray didn't like this Richard as much as he thought he did. He should have left five minutes ago, left this whole pathetic scene behind and driven to class and talked it out with someone, who undoubtedly would say they would have done the same thing. People always said that. Don't feel bad, I would have done exactly the same thing. I too am a coward. I too am a dog killer and live with the guilt on a day-to-day basis.

Ray held out his hand, and Richard gave him the phone.

"Hello?" Ray said. "Janet?"

"This is Janet," Janet said.

She actually sounded like a very nice woman. Ray had expected a screaming wench. He breathed a sigh of relief.

"I'm Ray," he said. "Listen, I don't know what Richard told you."

"All Richard told me is that there was something I needed to know and that you were going to tell me what that thing was."

"I see," Ray said. "So you have no idea—

"What this might be about," she said. "None."

161

Ray shot a death glance at Richard, and sighed. He didn't want to do this, again—once should be enough. But he had to remind himself that he was on the telephone; this was not a real confrontation. Everything was easier on the telephone.

"It's about K-9," Ray said.

There was silence. He kind of thought she might say something but she didn't, she didn't make a sound, and so it was quiet two or three beats longer than it should have been.

"Still there?" he said.

"I'm here," she said, her voice considerably diminished.

"K-9 ran out in front of my car this morning," he said. "It was completely unavoidable."

"What was?" she said.

"The accident," he said. "There was no way I could have avoided it. I'm sorry."

"Sorry?" she said. "Sorry about what? What exactly happened to K-9?"

Her voice, sweet at first, took on an edge now. He had made it perfectly clear what happened and yet she refused to recognize it. She was making it difficult for both of them.

"He's dead," Ray said, Richard nodding for moral support on the step above him. "It was completely instantaneous, though, if that's any comfort. I'm pretty sure there was no pain."

"Oh, are you God?" she asked him.

"Am I God?" Ray paused, amazed. "No," he said.

"Then I don't know how you could know whether there was pain or not. How can you tell me that if you're not God?"

"What I *meant* was—" he said, but suddenly he was talking to a dial tone. She had hung up on him.

He looked at the phone and then handed it back to Richard.

"She hung up on me," Ray said.

Richard shrugged.

"She'll call back," Richard said. "She's cooling off. Meditating a little bit, trying to understand what happened. She has a habit of killing the messenger. A little problem, but she's working on it."

"I think I see why you're divorcing her," he said.

"I'm not divorcing her," he said. "She's divorcing me."

"Oh," Ray said, and nodded, waiting for this moment to pass.

"Well, I need to be getting to school," he said, taking a backward step or two.

"Without even showing me where Andrew is?" Richard said. "That's kind of a cop-out, isn't it?"

Ray stuck his hands deep into his pockets and sighed yet again.

"Okay. I'll show you."

As he turned to walk to the car, the telephone rang, but Richard didn't answer it. He held it out for Ray.

"It's for you," he said. "I'm sure of it."

Ray stopped, and took the phone, reluctantly, and Richard walked inside.

"Hello?" he said. "This is Ray."

"So," she said, "are you a friend of Richard's or something?"

"No," he said. "I mean, I just met him. I found the address on K-9's collar and came here to tell him what happened."

"Are you trying to rip the heart right out of my chest?"

Clearly, the moment of meditation hadn't done her much good.

"No," Ray said.

"Then why the telling detail? 'The address on K-9's collar.' I can just picture it. Thanks for the memory, Ray. Who the hell *are* you?"

"I'm Ray," he said.

"No last name?"

He almost told her, then paused.

"That's not important," he said.

"Last names are important," she said. "I'm getting ready to change mine. That's important. Who are you to tell me that last names are not important?"

"*My* last name isn't important," he said. "That's what I meant. I'm sorry about all this. I really am. It was an accident. But I don't think it's necessary to keep yelling at me."

"What else aren't you telling me?" she said.

"Nothing," he said.

"I mean, what is it you're *hiding,* Ray? If that's your real name."

"That's my real name. Why wouldn't I tell you my real name?"

"Did Richard hire you, Ray? Are you getting paid for this?"

"*What*?"

"Are you some kind of dog hit man?"

"This is ridiculous," Ray said, holding the phone away from his face.

"Because it would not be hard for me to believe that he paid you to kill K-9. Because he couldn't do it himself, even when he's drunk, which is most of the time. That—*arghh*! The good news here is that I'm divorcing him; the bad news—for you—is that I'm going to have to break your legs. So you can't drive around anymore killing little dogs!"

Her voice, though full of an almost incoherent rage, was breaking now, and Ray could hear tears inside the words she spoke. She probably would have gone on yelling at him, too, but had to stop, just so she could cry. He heard a muffled mournful moan in the background, and sobbing, but it sounded as if it came from a distance, as if she had dropped the phone and walked away.

"Janet?" he said. "Hello?"

She was there. He heard her breathing in short, rapid bursts, collecting herself.

"Stay *right* where you are," she told him. "If you don't, if you leave the scene of this crime, I will find you. I swear to God I will. This is a life we're talking about. So just stay there and take me to K-9. Okay, Ray?"

"Okay," Ray lied, and they both hung up.

When Richard came back out Ray handed him the phone.

"Well, that's that," Ray said.

"So, how'd she take it?" Richard asked him.

"Not so well," Ray said, looking up to him. "Could have been worse, I guess," though he was having trouble imagining how.

"Believe me," Richard said. "It could have been *lots* worse. I have the paper cuts to prove it."

"Well, we better hurry," Ray said. "I want to show you where K-9 is, then I've got to go. I'm late to class already. My professor hates it when I'm late."

"I wish I had something to be late to," Richard said, laughing. "Like a job. I wish there was something else I could be fired from, but I've been fired from everything already. Job, marriage. All the biggies. You name it, I'm not doing it anymore."

Richard got in the passenger side, closed the door, and immediately the car began to smell like him, a mixture of sweat and pizza and beer and a half dozen other old things. Divorce was disgusting; Ray hoped it never happened to him.

166

Now that Ray knew the neighborhood better, Apricot, he realized, was just one street over, and he guessed that K-9 had come through his backyard, then through the neighbor's yard, and out into the street—probably on his way to visit a friend. Richard hummed and looked around Ray's car throughout the short trip, but stopped humming as they approached the still black form that was K-9 in the gutter ahead.

"Wow," Richard said. "That's—that's just *awful.*"

Ray nodded. There was nothing he could say now.

"I've really got to go," he said, looking in the rearview mirror. He didn't know where Janet had been calling from: she could be here any minute, he thought. And she was the last person he wanted to see right now. The absolute last.

Richard smiled and made a little sound with his mouth like *tsk.*

"She will find you, you know," Richard said. "I was listening in on the extension. She said she would find you and she will. That's the kind of girl she is."

Ray pretended not to worry, and gave the car a little gas.

"You make her sound sort of dangerous," he said, smiling.

"Well, let me put it this way: I'd move if I were you," he said. "Get out of town. Change your name, your identity, the way you look." Richard laughed and got out of the car. He peered back in before he closed the door. "Grow a mustache!" he said and laughed again.

Ray wasn't really worried. He was used to dangerous women. It's how he thought of them all.

167

SUMMER 1962

His Uncle's Ex-Wife

The day Ray's family moved, Bones ran away. His father dropped a lamp on his toe and both of them broke. Ray's mother almost cried walking from room to room, the echo of her heels making a sad sound, like nails dropping into a can. Then Eloise couldn't find the money she'd buried in the backyard a year ago, and she did cry, sobbing in the dirt with a plastic yellow shovel in her hands, surrounded by shallow holes. Uncle Eddie discovered a bed of snakes in a pile of old rags in the basement. Aunt Lurleen made a big plate of tuna fish sandwiches, and Ray found an old piece of paper with his secret name written on it. All this happened and it wasn't even dark yet, though you could see the moon, a pale sliver, in a corner of the sky.

After Ray's mother left with his dad for the hospital, Uncle Eddie brought one of the snakes up from the basement and set it on Aunt Lurleen's neck—a harmless little green snake, he said. He held its head while it wriggled across her nape, and Aunt Lurleen screamed. Ray had never heard anybody scream as loud as Aunt Lurleen did when she figured out it wasn't her husband's fingers but a snake that was on her. Turning, she lashed out with one of her arms and he dropped it, and Ray watched the snake glide off into the cabinet beneath the sink.

Aunt Lurleen ran out of the house and sat on the porch, in the porch swing, where she remained for some time. Uncle Eddie and Ray went out to look at her, but she ignored them. Her face was set icy tight. She didn't even blink. She wouldn't talk to Uncle Eddie when he apologized to her. She wouldn't talk to Ray, either, because he had been there and known what was going to happen and accidentally laughed about it. She just sat on the porch swing and trembled and stared across the street at the Seibal's azaleas.

"Lurleen," Uncle Eddie said to Ray in the kitchen, winking. "Lurleen, now, she has sure got a nerve problem." He picked up a tuna fish sandwich and bit at it. Then he looked at it. He looked at it as though it had bitten him.

"How about seeing if there's a beer in the fridge for me, Ray."

Ray found a beer, and he gave it to him. Uncle Eddie took another bite of the sandwich, chewed some and washed it down with the beer. He glanced out toward the porch. He looked like a man who really liked to eat.

Eddie was Ray's second uncle, having only just married Lurleen, his mother's sister, two months before. Ray hardly knew him, but he could tell by the way Aunt Lurleen acted when she introduced him that Ray was supposed to feel the same about Eddie as he had about his first uncle, Spencer, who had died in a car accident a couple of years before, when Ray was eleven. But it wasn't working out for Ray. It wasn't the same. Eddie was a small man without a hair on his face, his face was as soft and pink as a baby's, his eyes a deep sky blue. Sometimes it looked like there was nothing behind them, just that color. The hair on his head was thick and black, and he must have put something in it, because it was always shining. He was in the Navy for a couple of years, and got a tattoo while he was there, a eagle holding a bomb in its talons, wings spread across the top of his arm. Ray tried to imagine Uncle Spencer with an eagle on his shoulder and he couldn't. Uncle Spencer had to shave every day, and still his chin was so prickly when he rubbed it across Ray's belly that Ray almost died laughing.

"Your mom that way too, Ray?" Uncle Eddie asked him.

"What way?"

"Nervous," he said, wiping a bit of mayo off his chin with the back of his hand. "Jittery. On edge. Your dad sure gets on her nerves."

"No," Ray said, trying to think. What was his mother like? He couldn't say in words. "Not really."

"What?"

"Nervous."

"Is that so?"

"Well, maybe a little."

He smiled, liking that answer better than the other one. He had quite a smile. When he smiled his lips stayed together at first, until, parting slowly, he showed every tooth he had.

"I thought so," he said.

Uncle Eddie was a salesman until recently. He sold reproductions of the world's great art—and not on poster paper, but on hard, solid cardboard. He sold the frames, too. He'd carried it all in a briefcase that was four feet long, three feet high, and two inches wide. But he no longer did that. Ray was listening to him talking to his dad last night in the living room, packing, and heard him say that the company he was working for had become unreliable, unable to ship the great quantity of art he sold on time, or they were out of stock—just generally unreliable. He couldn't work for a company like that, so he quit, and he was between jobs now. But he had gotten to keep the briefcase full of samples, which was always in the backseat of his car, a lime green Dodge Dart. Just in case, Ray thought, he was suddenly possessed of the need to sell something.

"Why did your grandaddy name her Lurleen?" Uncle Eddie asked him, out of nowhere. "Where did that name come from?"

"I don't know," Ray said.

"Lur-leen," he said, drawing it out. "*Lur-leen.* Is it a family name? Is that the explanation?" He laughed. Then he winked at Ray. "I got pet names for her anyway," he said, almost whispering. "Don't use the Lurleen word much at all, actually."

She was still out on the porch. Her back was to them, but they could tell she hadn't changed a bit, that she was still staring across the street at the Seibal's azaleas. Ray could hear Eloise packing. Nothing was the way it was before. Even his dog was gone.

"I've got to go find Bones," Ray said.

Uncle Eddie looked at him. "Bones'll be back," he said.

"I think we spooked him," Ray said. "All the moving and packing. I've got to find him."

Still Uncle Eddie stared at him. It was like he didn't trust Ray, like he sensed that one of the things Ray was trying to get away from was him. Then his lips spread open to a wide-mouth smile.

"You mean *we've* got to find him," he said.

He jingled his car keys like little bells in his pocket.

"Let's go, sailor!" he said.

"But what about Eloise?" Ray said, following him out the front door.

"She'll be fine," Uncle Eddie said. "Lurleen can take care of her. Take care of Eloise, Lurleen," he said to her as they passed. Aunt Lurleen didn't move a muscle. Her eyes were like cold little marbles sitting heavy in her head.

"She's trying to remember why she married me," Uncle Eddie said, catching a glimpse of her through the rear-view mirror as they pulled away. "Sometimes it takes her a while. She'll be okay."

In the car, Uncle Eddie told Ray how much he liked to drive. He said he just loved it. He'd been about everywhere too, driving. Working. He used his thumb to point to the briefcase in back. This old Dart has been places! he told him. Oh yes! Driven to the edge of America, where the waves slap against the two-lane blacktop as it bends into the sea. Once he drove too close to the sun as it set, he said, burning the end of his nose. And he touched it like it still hurt a little. In the Navy he drove a forklift, and he got good at it, angling those rusty tusks into places nobody'd believe they go.

"I wish your Aunt Lurleen liked to drive," he said. "But she just about breaks down crying every time she gets into a car."

"Because of what happened to Uncle Spencer," Ray said.

He nodded. "That's right," he said. They were traveling about fifteen miles an hour down an empty street. "I think she'd rather ride on an elephant's back than get into a car. I

173

swear. But that comes from her nerves, and not having the best life in the world."

That was true. Ray's parents often talked about Aunt Lurleen and her awful life. Even before her first husband was killed in a car accident, she had been involved in a number of situations that, they said, always seemed to turn out badly. She had been robbed, her car had been vandalized. She had to sell her house to pay back taxes Uncle Spencer left behind. Bad luck and natural disasters seemed to follow her around. The day Ray's mother and dad found out she was marrying Eddie Del Vecchio, they just looked at each other and shook their heads, the way they did when other bad things happened to Aunt Lurleen.

"Eddie Del Vecchio," Ray's father said.

Ray and his Uncle Eddie drove around the block, looking. They passed the house, where nothing had changed. Aunt Lurleen was still on the porch. Uncle Eddie waved and Aunt Lurleen raised her hand slightly. That was a good sign, he said.

They kept driving. Uncle Eddie's car smelled like old rubber. "I don't see him," he said.

They drove around the block again, then around the next block, on a backstreet near the high school, but no Bones. Ray called to him from the window, but there was still no Bones.

"He'll be back," Uncle Eddie told him. "Don't you worry about that dog. Today, tomorrow, the next day. He'll be back."

"But we won't be there," Ray said.

"Oh," he said. "That's right. We should get back and finish up while your dad gets that foot fixed, shouldn't we?"

Ray said yes, he guessed they should.

But they didn't go back. Uncle Eddie said that as long as they were in this neighborhood they should go visit an old friend of his. More than an old friend, he said. She was family.

"And family's not like"—Uncle Eddie crinkled his eyes—"like a can of soup," he told him. "A family don't have an expiration date on it. Family is family forever whether you like it or not." And he gave Ray a wink.

They drove to the end of the good part of town or the beginning of the bad, it was hard to tell which. There was a chainlink fence around a small brown yard, running alongside a pale blue wooden house. The fence, Ray thought, was the nicest thing about the whole place. It looked strong and shiny where everything else looked scraped and torn. The little walkway leading up to the screen door was broken and grass shoots grew through it, and beyond the screen door it was so dark Ray thought there may have been nothing at all in there.

As soon as the car stopped out front a woman walked out of the house and stood on the porch. She was a big woman with brown hair hanging down to her shoulders, barefoot.

"She's nice," Uncle Eddie said, waving to her through his window. "She might not look nice from here but she is. Don't worry. You'll like her."

He grabbed Ray's knee and squeezed it, and with his other hand pushed his hair back.

Uncle Eddie was halfway up the walk before Ray got out of the car. Ray wanted to stay there, but the farther away Uncle Eddie got the harder it was for him to stay. The woman on the porch watched Ray come forward, and Uncle Eddie turned to grin and then Ray felt a strong urge not to be there.

"This here is Ray, my nephew," Uncle Eddie said to the woman, holding Ray by the shoulders in front of him. "Ray, say hello to Sally."

"Hi Ray," she said.

Ray said hello.

"Sally and I were married once," Uncle Eddie said. But it was like he was telling her that, and not Ray. Like she might not remember too well. "Before Lurleen, of course. Before Lurleen it was me and Sally. Three matrimonial years together. But then one thing led to another, right Sally?"

"I guess that's right, Ed."

She spoke as though the words were being taken from her, or barely escaping through a crack in her mouth. But Uncle Eddie was a salesman, and he kept trying to sell her. He kept talking.

"'Till death do us part,' I vowed," he said. "But we couldn't quite do it."

"Not for lack of trying," she said.

Uncle Eddie's grip on Ray's shoulders tightened. Ray could have been a piece of wood, a fence, or a tree.

"Now, Sally," he said, trying to keep it friendly. "That's all in the past, isn't it?"

"Feels like the present now."

Uncle Eddie laughed.

"I can't believe this," he said. "I come over to say hello and introduce you to my new nephew and here I am put through it all over again. Can't we just be like normal people and have a regular conversation?"

"I am a normal person," she said.

Sally had on a T-shirt with the name of a bakery on it, and white shorts that clung tight to her big legs. There was a bruise the color of dark water on one of her legs. She didn't look like anybody's aunt to Ray.

"Who's not normal?" he said and laughed. Then he was quiet. Then he said, "I guess you heard about me getting married, huh?"

"I think I might have," she said, sighing. "Maybe I read about it in the papers."

"It was in the paper?" he said, seeming genuinely excited.

"In the obituary section," she said.

"The obituary—what do you—"

Uncle Eddie's fingers dug into Ray's neck, and Ray thought, I have to go. But he continued to stand there between them.

"You know, I've got some art out in the car," he said. "Got some pretty pictures that might look good in your living room or foyer. One by Renoir I've got looks a lot like you, Sally. Care to have it? Gonna get rid of them one way or another."

Sally didn't even answer him. She just shook her head like she couldn't believe he would think of offering her some art. They stood there awhile longer, not talking. Sally hadn't moved since she came out of the screen door, and Uncle Eddie just held Ray out in front of him, hands on his shoulders, as though they were about to get their picture taken.

"What is it you want, Ed?" she said, finally.

"Want?"

"You didn't forget anything, did you? Pair of socks maybe? Something you need to come in and look around for? A book?" she said, and laughed.

"No," Uncle Eddie said, dropping his arms to his side now. "Me and Ray here, we're looking for a dog. We're looking for a dog, aren't we Ray? Ray's dog run away. You hadn't seen it, Sally, have you?"

"Nope," she said quickly.

"But we haven't even told you what it looks like!" he said.

"That's all right, Ed."

"He's dirty white," Ray said. "Medium-sized. With pointy ears. Named Bones."

"Sorry," she said, looking at Ray for half a second, then back at Uncle Eddie.

"Come on, Ray," he said. "Let's go. She's no help. She's no help at all, is she?"

Ray knew he wasn't supposed to answer that question. He waved to her, a flip of his arm, and turned and walked with Uncle Eddie back to the car.

THE SKY WAS DIM and orange. The road was dark beneath the trees. Some cars had their lights on already. Ray wished they were going home, but Uncle Eddie didn't want to go home just yet. Uncle Eddie wanted to drive. They weren't looking for Bones anymore. Bones wasn't a part of anything they were doing. Uncle Eddie was doing what he wanted to do.

"She wasn't very nice," Uncle Eddie said after a while.

"She seemed like she could be nice," Ray said.

"But she *wasn't*," he said. "She could have been but she wasn't. I'm sorry, Ray, sorry you had to see that."

They turned off the main road then and hit gravel. Uncle Eddie lost control of the car for a second, but then it righted itself. The wind was cooler here, and moist. Ray clung to the door handle. The trees bent low over the road, and kudzu grew thick around the branches. Ray couldn't say how Uncle Eddie saw ahead.

Uncle Eddie stopped in front of a big tree at the edge of the forest, its thick and gnarly branches spiraling out into the sky. He turned off the engine and said to Ray, "This is where I come to think." Then he reached into the backseat for his briefcase full of art and got out. Ray didn't move until Eddie stuck his head back in his window. "You coming?" he said.

There was a dirt trail winding through the forest, the trees covered with vines, and Ray followed Eddie down it. Eddie was walking fast, the briefcase banging against his leg as he went. Ray could hear a sound ahead of them—it was like static, he thought, and he imagined there was a television out there somewhere, in the middle of these woods, shining blue and gray. But it wasn't a television: it was a river, and the sound he heard was water falling over rocks and between logs. He could see it plainly by the light that fell through the opening in the trees above it—a river, not too many miles from his home, and he had never seen it. He had not even known it was here. Nobody had ever told Ray about it or brought him to it, not until Uncle Eddie did that night, and now Ray was moving away. They were moving. Not too far away, but too far to come back here. It was like it had been planned this way, like the river had been saved for the very last, when there was nothing he could do with it but remember.

Uncle Eddie was quiet as they sat there on the bank, the briefcase on the ground beside him. His face caught the sky light and drank it up. After a long time he spoke.

"Ever wonder where the stars go in the daytime, Ray?" he asked.

Ray shook his head.

He laughed softly. "If they was lightbulbs," he said, "somebody would have to go around and shut off every last one of them."

"They're not lightbulbs," Ray said.

"No they're not, Mr. Smart Guy. So where do they go?" he asked again.

"They don't go anywhere," he said. "The sun's just brighter."

"Correct," he said. "They don't go anywhere. The sun drowns 'em out." He looked up at them. "Hey, you're not going to tell Lurleen where we went today, are you?"

"I hadn't thought about it," Ray said.

He gazed toward the opposite bank.

"Well?" Uncle Eddie said.

"I won't tell her."

Uncle Eddie gave Ray his smile and nodded.

"You're okay, Ray," he said.

They sat there for a few minutes longer, until Uncle Eddie stood up with a groan and stretched.

"Watch this," he said.

He opened his briefcase and pulled out one of the

cardboard pictures. He took a look at it, squinting in the moonlight.

"Van Gogh," he said. "Van Goghs can really fly." And with a flick of his wrist he sent the picture flying over the river, disappearing into the trees on the other side. Ray could tell he'd done it before. He could tell this wasn't the first picture Uncle Eddie had sent flying.

Eddie reached for another. "Picasso," Uncle Eddie said. "Better than a Frisbee."

It wasn't really better than a Frisbee, Ray thought. It didn't fly straight, but it could go high and far, like a boomerang, only not quite coming back.

"Give it a try," Uncle Eddie said.

He handed one to Ray.

"Who is it?" Ray asked.

"Let's see," Uncle Eddie said. "I think—I think that's Caravaggio. You probably never heard of him. Note the use of chiaroscuro—how the light and dark come together. Great for the bath or hallway. Toss it."

Ray did, but it didn't make it to the other bank. The picture went almost straight up into the air and disappeared into the darkness of the sky. For a second Uncle Eddie and Ray both were looking straight up. It had disappeared. It was like some hand had come down and snatched the picture up. But then it came, cutting the air like hummingbird's wings, straight down out of the darkness, whirling and turning corner to corner so fast that it didn't seem to be turning at all. He could see the dark picture of the lady at the old oak table, a candle shining on one part of the small canvas, her deep white shoulder illuminated, her face lost in the shadows. Out of the sky it came, turning and turning and finally falling right on Uncle Eddie's forehead. It kind of stuck there for a second, and the sharp sudden pain of it knocked him down. He fell on the bank of the river and began to moan, holding his head with his hand, bringing it back stained with blood.

"Goddamn it!" he said. "Goddamn it! I hate art! *Hate* it!"

He stood up and kicked his big briefcase into the river, where it floated for a couple of yards until it snagged on a fallen branch. He stood there, enraged, breathing deeply.

After a while, he said, "Reckon we ought to be getting back."

Uncle Eddie drove slowly now. A little stream of blood, like a river on a map, had dried on one side of his head. Looking at it, Ray felt a little bit sick. But Uncle Eddie didn't say a word. He was like a stranger. Ray looked across the seat at him driving—the way his small hands clutched the steering wheel, the way his stomach fell over his belt just slightly—and wondered who he was. Nobody really knew, he thought—not even Aunt Lurleen. Or maybe she did, but Ray didn't think so. I might as well be with a man I never met, Ray thought.

"Jesus Christ," Uncle Eddie said, as they turned the corner to the street Ray lived on. "Look at that, Ray."

The lights from the car panned the house, sweeping across it like it was a prison yard. But the house was dark. The electricity must have been turned off already. Aunt Lurleen wasn't on the porch anymore, and Eloise wasn't there, and Ray's mom and dad weren't there either. The moving van was gone, too. Beyond the windows of all the rooms there was just black space, nothing there at all. And no Bones.

Uncle Eddie laughed as he pulled into the driveway, but it wasn't a good laugh. It was the laugh of a man who didn't have a better sound to make. The engine rumbled even after he turned it off. He got out of the car, leaving the lights on, and walked to the front door, where there was a note tacked, and he came back with it, waving it in the air like a little white flag. He got in the car and sighed, looking back and forth, from Ray to the note.

"They'll be back," he said. "Says they'll be back real soon." He stuffed the note in a pocket. "Says to wait right here."

"*Wait*?" Ray said. "We're supposed to wait for them here?"

"Sure," he said. "You don't believe me?"

"I believe you," Ray said.

"'Cause if you don't you can take a look at the note yourself."

"I believe you," Ray said. "I was just asking."

"Okay," he said.

He moved around in his seat, trying to make himself comfortable, and he yawned.

"Does it say anything about Bones?" Ray asked him.

He had to think about it for a minute, staring through the windshield at the house, still glowing in his headlights.

"It sure does," he said. "Now that you mention it. Says they found him. Says they have him there with 'em and everything's okay." He looked over at Ray, to see if he bought it. "Good news, huh?"

"Good news," he said.

"Yes sir. Everything's just grand," Uncle Eddie said. "Everything's fine and dandy. Not a thing in the world to worry about. This is happy ending time."

Uncle Eddie laughed and winked and hit the lights, and it was all darkness then, except for the stars. He turned the radio on low, almost too low to hear at all, and the dial glowed a sweet pale green. For a while he just sat there, staring out into the night. Then he closed his eyes, and his head fell back against the seat, his mouth just barely open, breathing deep and regular. Soon he was snoring, sound asleep. Ray watched him. Ray thought he looked like somebody who would sleep in his car. He looked like somebody this had happened to before.

FALL 1961
Inheritance

All the way to his grandfather's funeral, Ray stared out the window and watched the world go by, the long and lovely fields where they grew tobacco, the corn stalks tall and lazy, the old brown barns broken and ruined in the sun. There wasn't a cloud in the sky that he could see, and there were places on the vinyl seat too hot to touch, because of how bright and strong the sun was shining, even with the air-conditioning on. Eloise sat beside him and read. It didn't make her sick to read in the car, the way it did Ray. His father drove, and his mother sat in the passenger seat, her big black sunglasses covering up her eyes and her cheeks, and her light red hair pulled back and fastened flat against her neck with a tortoise-shell barrette. It was her father who had died. Occasionally, she would turn her head just slightly and say something to her husband, and he would look at her and nod, or just reach over and touch her on the shoulder. The hum of the road was like a sound barrier between the front- and backseats, so Ray couldn't hear what she said, or what his father said back, if anything. He just knew that they were being as nice to each other as he thought he'd ever seen them be, and, though Ray was only eleven, he knew this had mostly to do with his grandfather's death. This made him happy, though he knew he shouldn't be under the circumstances, but he couldn't help it. He was happy on the way to his grandfather's funeral.

"How are we doing back there?" his father asked after a while. There had been no fights, no territorial skirmishes, just the quiet of their bodies breathing, and the dry scratchy sound of another page turning. This in itself was worrisome to his father.

"I think I'm about to throw up," Ray said, making contact with his father's eyes in the rearview mirror. "All over you."

"I wouldn't do that," his father said. "You know, there's a Little Boy Swap Shop around here somewhere. Up the road about a mile. It may be time to turn you in and get a newer model."

"Yeah, right," Ray said.

"They make 'em now so they don't throw up," his father said. "They even have a special model—the RQ909—that never talks back, and if you want him to do things like his chores or his homework you only have to ask him once."

"Probably couldn't afford it," Eloise said, without lifting her eyes from the page.

"Hey," his father said, whose financial standing in the world was not what it once was. "They have a Little Girl Swap Shop, too, you know."

"Yeah," Eloise said. "But why trade in something that's perfect already?"

Ray wished he'd thought of that.

"Good point," his father said, and he caught Ray's eyes again. "But as for you, my boy. The RQ909 is a definite possibility."

"Do you think joking around like that is a good idea?" his mother said. They'd been joking around like this forever; Ray wondered why she'd chosen now to notice. "I mean, it might give him a complex or something."

"A complex," his father said. "What's a complex?"

"A problem later in life," she said.

"We all have problems later in life."

"Still," she said, but gently, without the passion she usually brought to her objections.

"Is there a Husband Swap Shop?" Eloise said, lifting her eyes to show their glimmer. "Maybe we should stop off there."

Their mother and father looked at each other.

"Yep," their father said. "There is one around here somewhere."

"Then there must be a Wife Swap Shop, too!" Ray said, excited by his foray into cleverness.

"Oh, but there's not," his father said, and he reached across the car to rest his big hand on his wife's thin shoulder. "A woman may have many husbands, but a man will always only have one wife."

POPS HAD BEEN SICK a long time before he died, so long, in fact, that by the time he eventually succumbed there was a greater sense of relief than of sadness. Ray and Eloise had been prepared for months. "Pops is really, really sick," they were told back in March, and here it was August they were making the three-hour drive from Birmingham to Atlanta. In a way, he had died and become a memory in their minds already, and going to the funeral was a kind of belated observance of the fact. Ray and Eloise would have spent a week with them in June, had he not been in the hospital, and now that he was dead these trips would stop forever. Grammy was going to be moving to Birmingham, to live in a rest home.

Ray had one very special memory he clung to, cherished even. Pops had many ways of entertaining Ray and Eloise when they came to visit. He did magic tricks sometimes. He knew what card you were going to pick before you even picked it. He made little green balls fly from one hand to the other. And he had a way of sticking a silken handkerchief in his hand and making it disappear completely. His old hands, so small and brittle and blue, shook as he stuffed the red handkerchief into his clenched fist, waving his other hand magically above it saying "Abra ... cadabra!" He even had a dinosaur bone, and a box with some of the hair from a horse he rode into Mexico, chasing Pancho Villa, the bandit.

But the thing Ray longed to see was his penny. Pops always kept it in his pocket, in a thin plastic case so it wouldn't get worn. There was nothing like it for Ray, that penny.

"This," Pops would say, holding the coin in its case as Ray sat in his lap encircled in his arms, "is an authentic 1909 VDB-S penny. They used to make pennies with Indians on them before this, and they're called Indian Head pennies, but this is the first one they made with a picture of Mr. Lincoln, our sixteenth president, on it. I did not know Mr. Lincoln, Ray, I'm not quite that old, but I once sat in a chair he sat in, and it was *still warm.*" Pops always laughed at this, and Ray always smiled. "At any rate. This penny was designed by a Mr. Victor David Brenner. I may have told you that before." (He had told him fifty times at least, maybe more.) "That explains the initials, VDB. And these first pennies were made in San Francisco, way out in California. That explains the S. Great weather out in California, Ray. Even when it's winter here, it's warm in California. But anyway, you know, Victor David Brenner only had a few of these pennies made with his initials on them as big as they are here, Ray. You can see it clear as day: VDB. I don't know how many they made for sure, but I can tell you, a very very few. *And this is one of them!* What you're holding in your hand is almost as rare as that dinosaur bone. It's just, you know, a lot smaller. A penny is one of the smallest things. People talk about getting rid of them, because of that. Rounding up. But I don't think it's a good idea to get rid of something just because it's small, do you?"

Ray shook his head.

"Because you can't round up," he said. "Not really."

Then he would look all around to make sure they were alone, and he'd whisper in Ray's ear, "Now, can I tell you a secret?"

Ray nodded, even though he told Eloise almost everything.

"This is just between you and me and the lamppost, okay?"

"Okay."

"One of these days," he said, "this penny: it's yours."

"Mine?" Ray said softly.

"Didn't I just say that?" he said.

And Ray thought, Mine! Mine!

This was what Ray was thinking about on the drive from Birmingham to Atlanta; when people died, they usually gave some of their things away to people who were still

living. Eloise had always admired the disappearing handkerchief. Maybe she'd get the handkerchief. But Ray was
getting that penny.

THEY DIDN'T GO TO Pop's house when they drove
into Atlanta: they drove straight to the funeral home. It was
a low brick building on the side of a small road, not far
from the cemetery, and as they pulled into the parking lot
Ray noticed his mother's shoulders start to shake.

"Sweetheart," his father said, and reached over and
touched her, and when he did she sobbed. Eloise and Ray
looked at each other, their expressions blank and muted.

"I know, I know," his mother said, taking a deep
breath, seeming to steady herself with a hand on her husband's shoulder. "I can do this."

"You can," his father said. "We know you can."

She wiped her face with a tissue without removing her
sunglasses, and said, "I'm okay. I really am."

There were lots of old people at the funeral home.
Some brought umbrellas, which Ray thought was funny,
because it wasn't raining. There were only six or seven cars
in the parking lot. Ray's father turned around to face his
children.

"What we're going to do," he said, "we're just going to
go in there to see Grammy and hug her and tell her we love
her. That's what all these people are doing here. Just telling

her how much they loved Pops. Then, if you want, we can go into the room where Pops is and say good-bye to him."

"Where Pops is?" Eloise said, uncomprehending.

Eloise looked at Ray and Ray looked at Eloise, their eyes wide in amazement.

"You didn't *tell* them?" their mother said to their father.

"I thought you—"

"As if I didn't have enough on my mind," she said.

"Okay, okay," he said, and he breathed once and looked away. "Sometimes, at things like this, the person who died, he's in a special room in, you know, his casket, and people who want to can see him there and see that he's dead and know it and then remember him the way he was alive."

"He's on *display*?" Eloise said, and she started crying, too, and her mother's hand reached around the seat to hold her, and Ray's father pursed his lips and shook his head, and looked at Ray with a helpless, hopeless expression.

"You should have told them," his mother said.

IT WAS TRULY AWFUL inside the funeral home. It was like a library. Grammy sat on a bench by herself. Ray had never seen her like that before, alone. Her eyes were red and her face was withered and when her daughter walked in Ray couldn't explain what happened to Grammy's face, exactly, but it seemed to explode in tears. They embraced.

Ray's dad stood back a little with Ray and Eloise, neither of whom knew how to act or what to do. Grammy saw them over their mother's shoulder, and walked over, trying to smile now, and hugged them both at the same time.

"My babies," she said, and that was all.

Then Ray's father hugged her, and then Grammy took Ray's mother's hand and together they walked into the room.

"That's the room," Eloise whispered to Ray.

"I know," he said.

"He's in there."

"I *know*."

"Are you—"

"Are you?"

They looked at each other, neither willing to commit.

"I'm afraid I'm *accidentally* going to look," Eloise said. "Let's sit where we can't even accidentally look."

So they moved backward a bit, and sat in some fold-out chairs against the far wall.

This room wasn't too crowded. Most of the people who had wanted to see Pops had already done so. Ray's family was among the last there. Ray could see through the glass doors of the funeral home how the sun was breaking up through the tree tops. Soon they were going to have to go back to Pops's house, where there was no Pops, and sleep. It would feel funny, Ray thought, not to sit in his lap again, not to be encircled by his arms, not to see the penny. It would feel really funny.

Finally, Grammy and their mother came out of the room. Ray thought his mother looked a little better, somehow, and Grammy did, too. Her face wasn't as bunched up as it had been. As she got closer she looked like the way he remembered her, bright-faced.

"It means so much just to have you here," Grammy said to them. "Pops loved you so much. You know that, don't you? He loved you so much." She looked like she was about to start crying again, but Eloise reached out and rubbed her shoulder, and she stopped. "He had some things, some little things, that I want to give you. I know he wanted you to have them. Eloise," she said, and she reached in her pocket and pulled out the magic red silk handkerchief. "You know what this is, don't you? I don't have to tell you what this is. I want you to have it. He wanted you to. And Raymond," she said, reaching in her other pocket. "This is for you."

She handed him the dinosaur bone that Pops had said was part of a femur.

"I know you loved that," she said, crying freshly now, as though for the first time. "I know you loved it, and it's like a part of him." She tried to laugh. "He was kind of an old dinosaur himself, wasn't he?"

"Yes ma'am," Ray said. He looked up at his father, who was urging him on with his eyes. Ray got the message. "Thank you."

"Thank you," Eloise said, and wiped a tear away with the magic handkerchief.

"But, what happened to the penny?" Ray asked.

He tried to ask in the right way, so that it didn't sound as though he wanted the penny more than he wanted the dinosaur bone, and he was partially successful. Only Eloise knew his heart.

"You sweet thing," Grammy said, and reached down to hug him yet again. "You know, a day didn't pass Pops didn't have that penny in his pocket. Not a day. It was like his lucky charm, I guess. He didn't feel right without it. So I felt like we should let him take it with him. They say you can't take it with you, but when your old Pops makes it to Heaven, I bet he'll persuade St. Peter. It's just a penny, after all."

But Ray still didn't get it.

"So . . ." he said.

"It's in his pocket," she said.

"In the room," Eloise said to him.

Ray held the femur in his hand for a moment, and he looked down at the floor, letting a respectable amount of time pass before he looked up again.

"May I go in?" he said.

His mother and his father and his grandmother all looked at the little man who was growing up in front of them, and Ray could see it in their eyes: they were proud. He was doing the hard thing, and they were proud of him. Only Eloise knew. She just said, "Ray."

RAY WENT INTO THE room alone. It wasn't such a
large room and so it didn't take as long to get to the casket
as he had thought and part of him hoped that it would, but
before he knew it, he was standing there, looking at his
grandfather. And it wasn't so bad, really. He had seen Pops
like this before, on the couch in his den, sleeping in front of
the television. But then Pops's mouth had been open, and
he could hear him breathing, and his body made little
shaky jumps, as though he were being pinched. In the casket, he was completely still and kind of wooden. Waxy, too,
and smaller than he remembered. But he had always been
a small man. Ray would be bigger than he was in a couple
of years, so the days of sitting in his lap with his arms
around Ray's waist were going to be over soon any way
you looked at it. Days when he would rub his grizzled
cheek against Ray's neck until Ray collapsed in manic
laughter. Days when he'd say, "I think you dropped a
freckle," and pretend to pick one up off the floor and replace it on Ray's arm. Days when he let Ray steer his truck
down the gravel road, sitting close beside him.

Ray looked at his dead grandfather, but nothing happened inside. Ray didn't feel the way his grandmother or
his mother did. He didn't know why, but he didn't. He didn't
feel like crying. But his heart beat faster than he thought
possible. He wondered if he was having a heart attack.
There was no one in the room with him, no one but Ray

and Pops and the lamppost. And he saw where the penny was. It made a little wrinkle against Pops' trousers. He slipped his hand across his grandfather's body without touching it—he didn't want to touch it—and into his grandfather's pocket, where it was cool, not like a real pocket at all, and he took the penny, still in its plastic case, in his fingers, and clutched it in his hand, and he stuck it into his own pocket, and it was done.

THE REST OF THE day, that night, and the next day went by without Ray paying that much attention. He had the penny, and the penny, in a way, had him. They were in this together now. It was what he thought about, what he felt, what he alone in the world knew. He had the penny. It was not something you could tell anybody, though, even though there was nothing wrong with what he had done, and the fact of this made Ray feel special and alone.

Later, he would remember certain scenes from those two days with a caustic brightness, as though he were viewing photos from an experience he mostly missed.

He remembered going to Pop's house after the funeral, and what it was like without Pops there but having the penny anyway, which he thought was kind of like having Pop there, because the penny was so much of what Pop was to him and having it was like having him there. Maybe that's why everybody else was so much sadder than he was. He was fine. He remembered going to sleep on the floor in the room his parents slept in, in the sleeping bag he'd brought with him, the penny still in his pocket, and waking up when his parents came in, and watching them undress to their underwear and climb into bed. It was like a dream. Ray didn't know if he was awake or asleep. His parents talked softly. He remembered his father saying how things were going to work out one way or the other, and his mother saying how that was no help: things always work out one way or the other. And his father said, "Exactly." But they held each other that night—Ray saw it—and he went to sleep with that picture of them in his head, holding each other, until he woke extra early the next morning, thinking of the penny.

He remembered the funeral, or parts of it, the long dull speech by the pastor, the terrible quiet, the hole in the ground. He remembered the tie he was forced to wear, and how it almost strangled him. And, of course, he remembered how the casket was lowered into the ground, and how everybody filed past and threw a handful of dirt down there. Ray threw in the dinosaur bone. He thought of it as a kind of trade.

All the way home, Eloise looked at him as if she knew. But Ray would not tell even her.

HE WOULDN'T TELL ANYBODY, ever. He would keep the penny in his pocket from then on, every single day, just as Pops had. It became his lucky charm, too. He would touch it whenever he felt like he needed something special, luck on a test, for instance, or the nerve to say something to a girl. He kept it in its plastic case so it wouldn't get worn, but then the case began to cut at his thigh when he ran. So he took it out of the plastic case and kept the penny, by itself, nestled in the lint in the bottom of his left pocket. Everything else went into his right. This was a 1909 VDB-S Lincoln head penny. He consulted a coin book and discovered that it was quite valuable, for a penny. In fine condition—and Ray thought his was in fine condition—this one penny was worth over twenty dollars. One penny. This amazed him.

The penny was now a part of Ray. Every night he placed it back in its case, and every morning he stuck it in his left pocket, where he could feel it, and know it was there. And maybe it was his imagination, but things seemed to go really well for Ray there for a while, even his parents were happy, until somehow—and he would never be sure how this happened, but it was bound to, he thought later, he should never have taken it out of its case—he lost it. He didn't know, but he thought it somehow got mixed up with his other, regular money, and he accidentally spent it, needing a penny to make his change come out right. Ray pictured how it must have happened, the penny leaving his very own hand and going to another, and then another, moving through the world now as though it knew where it was going, all the way to California, maybe, where it was warm, even in winter.

SUMMER 1960
A Good Deed

When the baby was born, the one thing Abby, Lilly, Mitch, and Ray wanted to know was, did it have a glass eye? The baby's mother had a glass eye, so naturally they wanted to know if the baby had one, too. Because it wasn't clear whether you were born with a glass eye or you got one, somehow, later. They all had an idea which it was, but no one really knew. Seeing the baby would be proof.

The lady with the glass eye was very kind and pretty and unlike anybody they had ever known. She had long brown hair, and she let it fall down her back, around her shoulders, wherever it wanted to go. And she had them call her by her name, *Nancy,* instead of Mrs. Branscombe, or Miss Branscombe, which, since she wasn't married, is what her name would have been. She was an odd lady like that.

They watched her move in, and she invited them over. The first thing she said after "Hello" was, "Who's who here? Who's who?"

She asked them in and gave them some water, and then, later, she showed them her eye.

If she had been ugly and known to have the glass eye, too, or if she had been cold and mean, her house without a doubt would have been like the witch's place, scary, the doorsteps they would have dared each other to touch. But she was pretty, and very nice, and brought their attention to her glass eye the day they met her. She said the eye was a gift, a gift from a king—the king of Brundai. She rested her hands on her stomach when she said this, her stomach already swollen like a balloon, and smiled. "Another gift," she said, "from the king." The next time she told them it came to her in a dream, that she dreamed her glass eye into her head. One day she said that it was magic, that it could see things other eyes couldn't.

Finally she told them that she was born that way, that her mother had a glass eye, and that her mother's mother had had a glass eye, too, that it was her inheritance.

She took the eye out and showed it to them that first time they came over. After that, she only took it out for them if they begged her long enough. And they begged. They begged and she let them have it.

Ray didn't beg so much; he left that to Abby and Mitch. But he held it when his turn came, this small piece of glass with the picture of an eye on it, and he would look back at her face and think, This is the thing she keeps in the place she kept her eye. The thought made Ray swallow. Because he thought it might be the same as holding any other part of someone's body in your hand—like somebody's heart, he thought, still beating.

EVERY DAY THAT SUMMER it was the four of them: Abby, the oldest, Lilly, her sister, Mitch, and Ray. Eloise was off at camp. Their houses formed a triangle in the neighborhood. They'd meet in the lot between the three, and then decide what to do from there. Much of their time they spent in the Swamp, or what they called the Swamp, but what was really only some trees around a stream. They thought of it as their place.

It was there Abby had the idea about the baby, and the eye, and what they would have to do to discover the truth. Ray listened, and, like Lilly and Mitch, nodded.

"WE'LL JUST SIT HERE and wait," Abby said.

Some days after they knew the baby was born, the four of them sat there and waited. This was no secret, that Nancy's baby had been born. Ray overheard his mother talking to Mr. Staples, their next-door neighbor. Mr. Staples had taken her to the hospital the day before. So they sat on the curb across the street from her house and waited for the baby. They didn't even knock on her door. They had always knocked on her door, and she had always come to it, but there were reasons why they didn't knock now. There were reasons why they sat there and waited.

For one, their parents told them not to bother her because she had her hands full, she didn't need the company. She didn't need the company anymore because now she had the baby.

But there were other reasons, too. Ray could hear it in his parents' voices. She was a mother without a man; it was a baby without a father.

Abby explained Nancy's situation to them. "If you get on a train," she said, saying something she'd heard her father say, "don't be surprised if you go on a trip." And, "She'd been around the block and seen a little smoke."

And so they sat on the curb across the street from her house and waited. Ray thought she would show them the baby the same way she showed them her eye, that first day.

"Want to see something really neat?" Nancy had said.

Lilly had been staring at her face. Lilly could tell there was something off-center about it, and had stared hard at it with her head cocked to one side, like a dog does hearing a high-pitched, far-away sound.

"It's kind of weird," Nancy said. "You want—"

"Yes!" Abby said. "What?"

"You're not going to believe it," Nancy said.

"I'll believe it," Lilly said. "*What*?"

Mitch and Ray didn't say a word. They looked around to see if they could find what it was she wanted to show them before anybody else did, but they didn't see it.

"It's my eye," she said. ""My left eye. Look at it. Close. See?"

"It's different," Lilly said, and the rest of them looked to see that it was indeed different from the other.

"That's right," Nancy said.

"So?" Abby said. She frowned and looked around for something better than just an eye that was different.

"So it's not real," Nancy said. "It's made of glass."

"Is not," Abby said. "That's stupid. There's no such thing—"

She stopped talking to hear Nancy's fingernail tapping against her eye. Ray heard it, the tapping sound *against her eye,* and almost felt the pain himself. He felt it the way Nancy obviously didn't, and that made it all the worse. She didn't feel it. This took his breath away.

"It's okay," Nancy said. "It doesn't hurt."

"It doesn't?"

"It's made of glass," she said. "It can't hurt. That's what's so neat about it."

They all stared at the eye, pushing each other out of the way to get a closer look. A glass eye was about as neat a thing there could possibly be, Ray thought, better than false teeth or a wooden leg. But the idea of it was almost too much to bear.

"Where did you get it?" Lilly asked her, like Nancy had gone out and bought it somewhere. "I mean, how?" she said.

"The king of Brundai gave it to me," she said, and then her glass eye seemed to sparkle. "I'll never forget the king. How could I? We met in the desert, under the sun. The sun is so bright and strong in Brundai that you can bottle the rays and open the bottles up at night to see by, like flashlights. Which is what they do in Brundai. Anyway, it was under this sun that we met, and it was love at first sight. But all that really means is that somewhere in the world there is someone for everyone to love—one person, it's a fact— and all you have to do to know it is to see him, and for him to see you. It was a one-in-a-million chance, of course, that I happened to be on the same stretch of desert where the king was, and that he took a moment to look down at the woman beside him. But he did, and we fell in love. And yet—are you listening?—I was a foreigner, and he had a kingdom to run, and we both knew there would never be any kind of future for us. We knew we could never marry. But our love was so strong we knew we could never live completely apart. So he gave me this eye, and I gave him mine, and when I look through it, through his eye, I see what he sees, and when he looks through mine he sees what I see. It's the only way we can be together. We see our lives as we're living them. In fact," she said, leaning down toward us, whispering, "he's probably looking at you right now!"

Lilly gasped, and waved.

"Right," Abby said. "Like I believe you."

"I see camels," Nancy said, dropping the lid on her good eye and staring off toward the ceiling with the other. "I see the sun and a man, an old man, sitting cross-legged on a corner in the bazaar, begging for change. The king walks among his people daily. He is concerned over the state of his kingdom. Not that it will ever disappear, but it could always be better. He always wants it to be better. I see . . . I see his wife, a woman he married not so long ago now. His wife is quite beautiful, the daughter of a wealthy family. The marriage had been decided upon at their births, they had always known, both of them, and yet—there is no love between them. None. The king loves me. Me. It's a sad story, isn't it?"

"Story is right," Abby said. "Let's go."

"Wait!" Nancy said. She said it like she really didn't want them to go. They were already following Abby toward the door. "I can take it out."

They stopped.

"Out?" Ray said.

Nancy took out her eye and gave it to him. Her lid closed down on the empty space, like one long wink.

Ray held it, and then they passed it back and forth between. It was something precious. It was Nancy's eye.

Then Abby pretended to almost drop it.

"Oops," she said. "Just kidding."

Nancy flinched.

"You," she said, smiling, and took the eye away and put it back in her face.

THEY WAITED. THEY WAITED for days. It would have been easy if, like most mothers, Nancy brought the baby out a lot. The weather was all blue skies, and town was just down the road. She could have taken it so many places and stopped off to show them as she passed. But she never brought it outside.

The more Nancy hid the baby, the more sure they were that they were right. She would bring the baby outside if it was a regular one, Abby said. If it was normal. If it didn't have a glass eye.

On the third day Mitch's feet got bitten by ants. Mitch didn't wear shoes, and there were ants in the gutter no one was looking to see, and while they sat there the ants bit Mitch's feet. The next morning he couldn't walk, his feet hurt so much. That was just as well, because something had happened to make Abby hate Mitch. Lilly and Ray didn't know what it was, but they didn't mind much either.

By the fourth day of looking at the dark house, waiting, Abby became pretty sure that something was up inside. Abby had asked her mother about Nancy and why she was keeping her baby locked up inside, and her mother had told her, "She's a little embarrassed, honey, that's all. She's embarrassed."

She was embarrassed because the baby had a glass eye.

Because it was one thing for *her* to have one, Abby reasoned, but it was altogether another for her *baby* to have one, and so it made sense that she didn't want anybody seeing it for a while, a few weeks—maybe forever. Maybe she was too embarrassed ever to let the baby see the light of day. Maybe Nancy was never going to let the baby out. Lilly wasn't sure about the glass eye, she had her doubts, and Ray said it must be something else, because babies, he said, weren't born with glass eyes. He had been asking people himself, and everybody said the same thing. Babies weren't born with glass eyes.

"Of course they're not," Abby said. "You're such a dork, Ray. That's why she won't bring it out. Because it's weird, get it? Get it, you idiot? Because regular babies don't come that way. You're stupider than Mitch. Fatter, too. You're fatter and stupider than Mitch. Congratulations."

BY THE FIFTH DAY they had a new plan. One of them would just sneak over to the house and look in the window. Simple.

This was Lilly's idea. Lilly said you could probably tell from the window if the baby had a glass eye, and Abby had to agree. But Ray didn't think so. Ray said that even though they had been told not to bother Nancy, even though it was breaking a new rule, it would be easier if they bothered her just this once and broke the rule, because Nancy wouldn't mind, and who cared about breaking the rule anyway?

Abby said this was out of the question. She said it was out of the question, that Nancy might have been nice before the baby came, but that now she had a baby and (she was sure) one with a glass eye, too, and that no matter what she had been like before, everything was different now.

"Anyway," she said. "That's too easy."

So it had become a challenge. Seeing the baby was their new summer game.

"So go on," Abby said.

"Who?"

"You," Abby said, facing Ray. "It's your turn. Go on and come back."

"But I don't want to," he said. "It was Lilly's idea."

"*Ray,*" she said.

Ray went. There was a long line of weedy-looking trees separating Nancy's yard from another, and so he walked behind them until he came to the side of her house, where there was a door and a window. The window was open but the shades were drawn, and though he could hear Nancy moving around inside he couldn't hear the baby. He crept along that side of the house and moved around the corner, past a bank of bushes growing against the house. He was in the backyard then. There were two open windows there, but they were too high for him to look in. Along the other side of the house, he knew, was where the bathroom was, so he didn't even bother going there. He went back to the side door.

It was open. Not all the way, just cracked open enough to let some of the darkness from the inside out. He thought if he could get close enough to the crack he could see something worth the risk. He crept toward it very carefully, and was almost there when the baby started crying. It was like one long cry for help.

Ray turned and ran away from the house as fast as he could and back behind the weedy-looking trees to the curb, so out of breath that all he could do was shake his head when Abby asked him what he saw, and if he had seen what she wanted him to.

"You're really pathetic," she said. "I knew you wouldn't see anything. You're too fat. You probably didn't even look. You were probably too scared."

"I looked," he said. "I just couldn't see the baby."

"Did not," she said.

"Did too. The side door was open. I looked through the side door."

"The side door?" she said. Her eyes got big. "It was open?"

"It was cracked a little."

"Great," she said. "That's great."

"What is?"

"The side door," she said. "For a fat boy you did good. Now I've got another plan."

There were two things that had to happen for Abby's plan to work: Nancy leaving the side door open was one, and the other was her leaving the baby alone. Ray knew she wouldn't leave the baby alone, she wouldn't go out with or without the baby, so it was sleep they were waiting for, a nap. When Nancy took a nap Abby would go in through the side door and take a look at the baby, and then they would know.

It was really dangerous, she said, a really dangerous plan, so dangerous that on the day she was going to do it Ray and Lilly decided not to go to the curb at all but instead to wait for her in the Swamp. She would go the long way around and hide beneath Nancy's bedroom window and wait until she heard her sleeping. She would just walk in, look, and walk out. She would tell them what she saw. That was the plan.

Abby was about to leave them in the Swamp when Ray said, "How can we believe you? Why should we believe what you tell us is true?"

She almost hit him. But then she didn't. Then she left.

"WHERE *IS* SHE?" Lilly said about half an hour later.

"She said just to wait here," Ray said.

"We *are* waiting," she said.

"So we'll wait."

There were some salamanders and crayfish beneath the creek stones, and Ray and Lilly worked at catching them for a while. When he picked up a stone the creek got muddy and the crayfish and salamanders swam through the mess he made trying to catch them. If he didn't try to catch them, the creek stayed clear. But if he tried to catch them the creek got muddy and he couldn't see where he knew they were.

"I'm bored," Lilly said, after a while. "I want to go home."

"You can't go home," he said. "Abby'll kill you if you go home."

"So?"

"So you want to be killed?"

"She can't kill me. Bugs!" she said, slapping her arm.

Then they heard the branches rustle, twigs snap. Lilly stood up. Ray turned over one more stone and watched the mud run brown through the water. It was Abby. He could see her red shirt through the trees.

"Ray!" she yelled.

Something bad had happened. Ray knew it. As she came closer Ray could hear Abby crying. She'd been caught, Ray thought, and she was crying because she knew she was going to be in trouble, and that meant all of them were going to be in trouble, and it wasn't a good feeling for Ray, thinking ahead to trouble.

But he was wrong. She wasn't crying. It wasn't like that at all.

"You wouldn't *believe* me," she said, getting closer. "Ray wouldn't believe me. So believe me," she said. "You were right. So it *doesn't* have a glass eye. Look."

And Ray found out then something he would learn again, with time: babies aren't born with glass eyes. They get them, somehow, later. But he couldn't think about that now. The baby was crying. It was the baby who was crying, not Abby. Abby held it in her arms the way women did, like she knew how. Ray thought she had probably seen it on television.

"The baby's crying," Lilly said. "Poor baby."

"And both eyes," Abby said. "Not just one. Tears are coming out of both of them."

"Abby," Ray said. "Abby, this is terrible."

"The baby's crying," Lilly said. She said this over and over. "The baby's crying." She pursed her lips in a pout.

"What's so terrible?" Abby said. She had this adult way of pretending it was okay, that everything was not as truly bad as it really was. "What's so terrible? Nothing's wrong. The baby's fine. *Chris,*" she said. "I heard her call it Chris."

"You just took Nancy's baby," Ray said. "You can't just take a baby from somebody."

"She's probably still asleep!" Abby screamed at Ray. "She probably doesn't even know it's gone!"

Ray could tell Abby thought it had all gone wrong. She never yelled. All the bad things she said were said evenly, confidently, because she was the oldest and the strongest of them all.

Then she started crying.

"You wanted to *see* it," she said. "You wouldn't believe me. It's all your fault, Ray. You said I was a liar!"

Her face was full of tears, all wet and red. The baby stopped crying and stared at Abby for a second. Then he whimpered a few times until Lilly touched his head. Then the baby stopped.

Ray looked at him. Two eyes. Green. On his head, almost no hair at all.

"Let's take him to our house," Lilly said. We can keep him for a while. He's so *cute.*"

"Take him back," Ray said to Abby. "Take him back *now.*"

She looked at the baby then, afraid.

She shook her head.

"I can't," she said. "I'm not. I don't want to."

"You took it," Ray said.

"We can take him to our house," Lilly said.

But neither of them was listening to Lilly.

"You think she's still asleep?" Ray said.

Abby nodded. Her nose was running now, too.

"Stay here," Ray said. "I'll take him back."

"We're not going to take him home?" Lilly said as Ray walked away, holding the baby in his arms the way Abby held it.

As he walked through the woods the baby calmed down a little, and finally, as they broke into the light, it stopped crying altogether and slept.

LATER, WHEN HE WAS old, Ray would remember what it was like to be young, and how good it was to be too young to know how serious the world is, that the most serious thing, and the last thing a child learns, is just how fragile it all is. He could play in the street, not thinking about or even wondering what happened to children who played in the street when a car came tearing by. They were killed, of course. He would learn that later, but he didn't know that then. Getting killed, dying: what is that exactly? And what possible difference could it make to a summer's day? There was not enough room for thoughts like this. And to think of a baby, just one week old, being held in the arms of a fat, possibly slow-minded boy of ten, of a baby being taken through the Swamp and the trees around the Swamp, past the branches that could scratch him, over fallen trees covered in moss the boy might slip and fall on—to think of it, to think of himself doing the same thing ten, twenty, or thirty years later, filled him with fear, the kind that would have made him careful, the feeling an older person would have holding this baby in his arms, a baby whose mother would be losing her mind now, if she woke and realized her son was gone.

But Ray wasn't thinking. He was simply doing the right thing, and doing the right thing came to him as naturally as breathing. How could he have known that this was a talent that would be lost over time?

There was half a mile between the Swamp and Nancy's house, and a straight line to it. Ray walked the line.

Though there was a chance Nancy was still asleep, a chance he could replace the baby and leave without anyone other than the three of them ever knowing, he knew the chances of this happening were small, very small, and that more than likely something else, something beyond his ability to reckon would happen, was happening even now. In his mind he saw what was happening. It was a vision, a vision he would carry with him the rest of his life.

He saw Nancy waking, opening an eye. Stirred briefly from the powerful dream she was having, a good dream, she closes her eyes and tries to return to it. Or maybe Nancy doesn't dream at all, but instead sees in her glass eye the king's world, vast, the endless stretch of desert before him, the miles between him and the next town, because there is always one more town to visit, to inspect, each piece and parcel of his kingdom as precious to him as the golden city of Mundi, the shining city of Mundi. Nancy can't even look at the city she sees when he sees it, it's that bright, that fantastic. When he returns to Mundi she must return to her own life in her own dark house. She must look at her baby.

But the baby's gone. She wakes, goes to the crib, and sees—an impossible horror—that the baby is gone. The crib is empty. She can't even scream because the reality of this impossible horror is beyond her reckoning, too. It's beyond sound and tears and belief, for she knows what has happened: the king has come for his heir.

She knew he would come. She knew that sooner or later he would come for what was his. In Brundai they say a woman keeps a child for a man the way she would keep a plant: while he is away she feeds it, helps it grow. But it's a custodial privilege and nothing more. This he made clear to her. As much as he loves her—and he does, he does not need words to tell her so—there are more important things than love. Who needs the baby more— Nancy, or his kingdom? One woman, or a million people? The king's wife is barren, but even if she weren't, even if she could have a dozen children, he would want hers, Nancy's child, to take his seat on the throne, to rule this wondrous kingdom. And so the king has come and taken the child away. It was inevitable, a part of the order.

And so is Nancy's great sadness. She falls to her knees, shaking.

IN HER BACKYARD THERE was what might have
been a pile of pinestraw, or a gathering of leaves. It may
have been a compost heap, because Nancy did have a garden, and before the baby was born Ray and Abby and Lilly
and Mitch would find her out in it, doing something on her
knees with the plants and flowers. It was soft, and it seemed
for the moment secure. Here is where Ray placed the baby.

Why, at that point, he didn't simply turn and run back
to the Swamp he could never say. For that Ray, the young
one, is so long gone by the time he has the capacity to understand, a fossil buried beneath the time of his life, that
he's like another person altogether, a stranger.

So for whatever reason he doesn't turn and run away
but instead walks to the side door of Nancy's house and lis-
tens. And this may be all he had intended to do, to hear
Nancy sleeping, or not. Or not: to hear what a mother
sounds like when the thing she is the mother of, is gone. He
has an idea this is a sound like no other.

When he hears this sound, he steps inside.

Nancy is leaning against the kitchen wall, and in the
moment before she sees him, he sees her—shivering, wail-
ing with short gasps of air, not even crying, her eyes are dry,
even sleepy, she has clearly just gotten up and out of bed in
time to see what is no longer there. But then she sees Ray,
and smiles. She smiles, and her eyes grow happy, almost as
if any child, at such a moment, will do. She goes to Ray and

scoops him up in her arms, and though he doesn't know what to do—his arms just hang there at his side—he says the words his mother has said to him at such times, when he has felt something like he thinks Nancy must be feeling now.

"It's okay," he says. "It's okay."

Then he turns her around and walks her outside, into the backyard, past the high weeds and the shadows and into the sunlight, and points to the far edge of her kingdom.

She raises her head, and Ray watches her go, watches her run to the baby who is waking now and crying, but all he can think about is her eye, and how cool it would be to hold it again, this piece of her, in his hand.

Ray In Heaven

Ray is back.

In the distance we see him, his dim figure walking slowly toward us. It's been some time since he's been gone; most of us had forgotten him, I think. People come and go up here. It's a mistake to get too attached to anybody. Still, I think I can speak for us all when I say how relieved we were to see Ray go when he did, storming off into the far reaches; his energy level was a bit high for us all. As he approaches the outer edge of the circle, a nervous shudder rolls through, and a hush falls, and all eyes go to him.

"Mr. Williams," Betty says, pretending to be pleased to see him. "What a surprise."

"A surprise?" he says. "What's the surprise?"

"We didn't expect you back."

"Oh," he says, and laughs a little, shrugging his shoulders. He looks worn out, and a little sad. "Well, here I am."

"We can see that," she says.

"I wandered around for a while," Ray says, rubbing his toes into the surface of the floor. "But I couldn't really find anybody. There's just a lot of . . . space, you know?"

"Really?" she says. "You didn't find any other groups?"

"Nobody," he says. "It got kind of lonely."

Betty nods and shifts in her seat.

"Lonely," Mr. Joyce says, as though he knows the feeling.

"I was sure there would be other groups where you'd be more comfortable," Betty says. "Perhaps I was wrong."

"No other groups," Ray says. "I think this is it."

Everyone looks at each other, exchanging puzzled glances. There are many other groups in Heaven—hundreds, perhaps more. Why he didn't find them is a mystery to us.

"I think," Ray says, after a moment of silence, "this must be where I belong."

"But by the way you acted before—"

"I'm sorry about that," he says. "I was a little upset."

Ray moves in closer, holding the backs of chairs for support. Though he has made his way back here to us, he still seems lost somehow, unsteady. When he looks at me— and he does, he finds me toward the back and I smile—he seems not to look so much at me, as through me, his eyes unable to settle on any fixed point.

"I don't know how hard I looked, really," he says then, staring toward the distance. "I was thinking a lot, wandering around. I couldn't stop thinking—you know."

"What?" Betty asks.

"My last words," he says. "They're like a song I can't get out of my head. The words just hang there."

"*I wish,*" Stella says, as though her participation at this juncture will raise her stock with the rest of us; it won't. "That's what you said, isn't it? *I wish.*"

Ray nods. You can look at him and see that he's still thinking about them, and nothing else, as if they've possessed him, not he them.

"Well, maybe it would help to talk about it," Stella says, and pats the empty seat beside her, inviting Ray to come sit.

"*Stella,*" Betty says, shaking her head. "We don't want to get into that here."

"For God's sake let the man talk," Stella says, rolling her eyes. "Let him get it off his chest. Then we'll all feel better."

Betty sighs. She looks at the rest of us, and takes a reading of our faces.

"Well, if it doesn't bother the others," she says, "then I suppose it's okay with me."

And nobody does seem to mind. We sit in much the same attitude we were in before Ray came back: quiet, our hands in our laps, waiting for the next one to speak. Ray moves slowly across the circle, and sits beside Stella Kaufmann, where he takes a deep breath. She touches his hand with her own, for encouragement, and smiles at him warmly.

He looks around at the group.

"Like I said," he says, "I've been thinking about it. *I wish. I wish. I wish*—for what? That's what started bothering me: I didn't know what for. What was I wishing for? I mean, I was fifty years old, and I was dying, and my wife was there, and my son was there, and they were waiting for me to die. And I hadn't been the best husband in the world, and I hadn't been the best father. And this was it: my very last moment. I felt like something had to happen then. Something that might explain it all to them, to me . . ."

"Well, that happens," Betty says. She looks at him, as if waiting for him to tell us just that.

Ray sighs.

"Then I remembered," he says, his face suddenly brightening. "I remembered what I was going to say, had I been able to say it. That's why I wanted to come back. To tell you. To tell everybody."

Which is touching, of course. Stella is especially moved. Her eyes are brimming with tears. But as for the rest of us, frankly, we've heard all this before. In fact, no one wanted to say this when he was here earlier, but have there ever been any more common last words than *I wish*? No, I'm afraid there haven't. *I wish* might actually be the chart topper. For what else does one have left to them at the end of an especially unproductive life—what, other than wishes?

And so I prepare myself, as I notice we all do, to feign an emotionally empathetic response when he tells us how he meant to tell his wife and son that he *wished* he'd been a better father, or that he *wished* he'd been a better husband, or that he *wished* he hadn't lied and cheated and used other people for his own selfish ends. It's always something like this, a great blanket wish for a great blanket of forgiveness.

But Ray surprises us.

"I wish," he says, "I had that penny."

FOR THE BEST IN PAPERBACKS, LOOK FOR THE

In every corner of the world, on every subject under the sun, Penguin represents quality and variety—the very best in publishing today.

For complete information about books available from Penguin—including Puffins, Penguin Classics, and Compass—and how to order them, write to us at the appropriate address below. Please note that for copyright reasons the selection of books varies from country to country.

In the United Kingdom: Please write to *Dept. EP, Penguin Books Ltd, Bath Road, Harmondsworth, West Drayton, Middlesex UB7 0DA.*

In the United States: Please write to *Penguin Putnam Inc., P.O. Box 12289 Dept. B, Newark, New Jersey 07101-5289* or call 1-800-788-6262.

In Canada: Please write to *Penguin Books Canada Ltd, 10 Alcorn Avenue, Suite 300, Toronto, Ontario M4V 3B2.*

In Australia: Please write to *Penguin Books Australia Ltd, P.O. Box 257, Ringwood, Victoria 3134.*

In New Zealand: Please write to *Penguin Books (NZ) Ltd, Private Bag 102902, North Shore Mail Centre, Auckland 10.*

In India: Please write to *Penguin Books India Pvt Ltd, 11 Panchsheel Shopping Centre, Panchsheel Park, New Delhi 110 017.*

In the Netherlands: Please write to *Penguin Books Netherlands bv, Postbus 3507, NL-1001 AH Amsterdam.*

In Germany: Please write to *Penguin Books Deutschland GmbH, Metzlerstrasse 26, 60594 Frankfurt am Main.*

In Spain: Please write to *Penguin Books S. A., Bravo Murillo 19, 1° B, 28015 Madrid.*

In Italy: Please write to *Penguin Italia s.r.l., Via Benedetto Croce 2, 20094 Corsico, Milano.*

In France: Please write to *Penguin France, Le Carré Wilson, 62 rue Benjamin Baillaud, 31500 Toulouse.*

In Japan: Please write to *Penguin Books Japan Ltd, Kaneko Building, 2-3-25 Koraku, Bunkyo-Ku, Tokyo 112.*

In South Africa: Please write to *Penguin Books South Africa (Pty) Ltd, Private Bag X14, Parkview, 2122 Johannesburg.*